'Going house-h...
luck.'

Ben was smiling ar... ... ...
in the clinic-room.

'Good luck,' Chloe called back. 'Hope you
find what you're looking for.' She unlocked
the car door and lowered the window.
'Well. . .goodnight,' she said lamely. What
else could she say? She had a feeling that he
was expecting something more. That he
wanted to engage her interest. Or was that
wishful thinking on her part?

Dear Reader

In Australia, Marion Lennox has Nikki and Luke find a STORM HAVEN; Laura MacDonald's Toni finds herself IN AT THE DEEP END with her new boss in Africa; at the health centre, Margaret O'Neill's Dr Ben Masters becomes NO LONGER A STRANGER to Clare Lucas; and we meet Michael Knight again— first seen in PRIDE'S FALL—in Flora Sinclair's KNIGHT'S MOVE as he meets his match in Jessica Balfour. Happy New Year!

The Editor

Margaret O'Neill started scribbling at four and began nursing at twenty. She contracted TB and, when recovered, did her British Tuberculosis Association nursing training before general training at the Royal Portsmouth Hospital. She married, had two children, and with her late husband she owned and managed several nursing homes. Now retired and living in Sussex, she still has many nursing contacts. Her husband would have been delighted to see her books in print.

Recent titles by the same author:

TAKE A DEEP BREATH
LONG HOT SUMMER

NO LONGER A STRANGER

BY

MARGARET O'NEILL

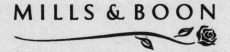

MILLS & BOON LIMITED
ETON HOUSE, 18–24 PARADISE ROAD
RICHMOND, SURREY, TW9 1SR

MILLS & BOON, the Rose Device and LOVE ON CALL are trademarks of the publisher.

First published in Great Britain 1995 by Mills & Boon Limited

© Margaret O'Neill 1995

Australian copyright 1995   Philippine copyright 1995 This edition 1995

ISBN 0 263 78917 9

Set in 10 on 12 pt Linotron Times 03-9501-53797

Typeset in Great Britain by Centracet, Cambridge Made and printed in Great Britain

CHAPTER ONE

WITH a sigh of relief, Chloe backed her white Peugeot into the car park and came to a halt in a pool of shade cast by the leaves of a massive chestnut tree. She felt unbearably hot and sticky, but then, according to the Met. office, it was the hottest May on record. She eased the dark blue cotton of her uniform away from her warm skin. Sweat was running down her neck and into the channel between her breasts. What she wanted most in the whole world, she thought, was a cold shower and a change of clothing.

So much for wishful thinking. It would be hours before she could shower and change out of uniform. She was on duty till six, perhaps longer, but at least the chestnut trees that lined the car park gave some temporary relief from the scorching heat. Their lime-green leaves hung motionless, but provided welcome shade. Their pink and white candles, standing erect on broad branches, seemed immune to the baking hot afternoon sun, which shone down relentlessly from a cloudless blue sky on the Chidhurst Health Centre. The car park shimmered in the almost tropical heat and little pools of bubbling tar gleamed in the fierce sunshine.

She glanced around as she dabbed at her hot face and neck with a refresher pad and then repowdered her nose, and added a touch of fresh lipstick. That was better; she felt a little more human. She noted that there were only a few familiar cars present in the staff parking area. Not surprising, as it was three o'clock, the 'dead' time of day at the centre.

There were a couple of cars belonging to the pharmacy staff on the far side of the park, together with Dr Alison Knight's dark blue Rover. Alison, Chloe guessed, would by now be in the middle of the antenatal clinic. Tucked away in a corner was, as always, Betty Box's Mini and, as always, Betty would be busy in Reception. In the nurses' parking area, next to Chloe's car, stood the red Fiesta belonging to Susan Ford, senior midwife, who would be assisting Alison in the antenatal clinic. The other parking spaces lay empty, as both medical and nursing staff were out making their various domiciliary visits. There was a scattering of cars in the patients' parking area.

A mid-afternoon golden hush lay over the sun-drenched health centre.

Chloe sat still for a moment, savouring the cool pleasure of the shade, and the faintest stirring of air through the open windows of her car. She was loath to move after her busy afternoon, and it was so peaceful here. She had no illusions; once she was back in her office she would be bombarded with messages and problems to solve.

Well, there was no reason why she should rush in. She could stay out here a little longer away from the telephone and other interruptions, and use the time to check over the notes pertaining to the home visits she had made. She opened the driver's door to let in a little more air, then pulled some cards out of her visiting case and became absorbed in them.

She had been working for some time when, with a swish of heavy tyres, a vehicle pulled in and stopped on the other side of the car park. Chloe looked up, expecting to see one of her medical colleagues in a familiar car, but was surprised to see instead a large Volvo estate that she didn't recognise, parked beside Alison's Rover.

A visiting medic? Possibly. Chloe glanced at the driver, who at that moment, perhaps sensing that he was being watched, turned his head towards her and gave a little nod, almost as if in recognition. She gave an answering nod. He was wearing dark glasses, and at this distance she couldn't see his features clearly. Was he a casual acquaintance in a new car, or possibly a rep who called at the centre occasionally? She couldn't be sure.

She watched covertly as, apparently deep in thought, he slowly removed his sunglasses, folded them with calm deliberate movements and tucked them into the breast pocket of his pale jacket. Even without his dark specs, Chloe didn't recognise him as someone whom she had met. And yet. . .did she know him? No, he had to be a stranger, a casual visitor, but there was something about him that was familiar, even at this distance. He seemed to command her attention and she found herself continuing to watch him surreptitiously as he unfastened his seatbelt and stepped out of the car. He locked the door and then, with long, easy strides, began to walk unhurriedly across the tarmac, a dark silhouette against the brilliant sunshine.

In spite of being certain that she didn't know him, as the man approached, Chloe experienced the most peculiar sensation of having seen him before. Surely there was something vaguely familiar about the very tall, broad-shouldered yet lean-looking man coming towards her. He drew closer, and now she could clearly see his strong features and well-cut dark hair neatly streaked with grey. Suddenly she realised why he seemed familiar. There was no question about it: this was the man whom her friend, the usually phlegmatic Susan, had described so enthusiastically. Sue's glowing description raced through her mind as she watched the stranger striding towards her.

'Talk about tall, dark and handsome,' Sue had said. 'He's all that and then some. It's not that he's conventionally good-looking: his nose is a bit too beaky for that. He's got a chiselled look about his face, and lines round his mouth, and he has piercing, steely grey eyes that look right through you. A bit unnerving really, and he looks rather serious and world-weary, but he's got a truly lovely smile that's quite something. He's no male model, but oh, brother, he's certainly all man, and he's got this lovely dark brown, velvety sort of voice.' She gave a theatrical sigh. 'If I were only a free woman, I could fall for our new doctor in a big way. What a pity you missed him when he came to look us over.'

'Well, I didn't go down with a tummy bug when he was due to visit just to avoid him,' Chloe had replied wryly. 'Anyway, I shall be seeing plenty of him in the future, since he's joining the practice. Though after what you've said, I can hardly bear to wait to meet this gorgeous hunk of manhood,' she had joked.

Well, she wouldn't have to wait any longer to meet the gorgeous hunk, she realised, for there could be no doubt that the man now approaching her was Ben Masters, Chidhurst's new doctor.

Automatically, conscious of feeling hot and untidy in spite of the repairs she had made to her make-up, she put up a hand and pushed back into place a golden tendril of hair that had escaped from her chignon.

He was almost upon her. He looked cool and immaculate in a stone-coloured, lightweight suit, and white, open-necked shirt that showed off the tanned column of his throat.

He smiled as he reached the car. 'Good afternoon,' he greeted her, in the deep, rich baritone that Sue had described as brown velvet.

Chloe, feeling at a disadvantage sitting down—he was so very tall—extricated her long legs from beneath the steering-wheel and got out smoothly before replying.

'Good afternoon.' She extended her hand to meet his. 'I'm Chloe Lucas. Can I help you?' She was conscious that she sounded stiff and formal, but she had no wish to let him know that she recognised him.

He took her hand in a firm, cool grip, and said with the same air of formality, 'Yes, I'm sure you can help. I'm Ben Masters—Dr Masters, due to join the practice tomorrow. How very appropriate that I should be welcomed by the centre manager.' He inclined his head in a little bow.

His immediate recognition surprised her. 'How on earth do you know who I am?' she asked.

His mouth quirked slightly at the corners, and he replied drily, 'Well, your name was a clue; it was mentioned when I came to look round, and I was told that you were the manager. And you were also described to me in some detail, and the description was so accurate and, dare I say it, properly flattering, that I recognised you directly I drew into the car park.'

Accurate and flattering! What had been said about her and by whom? That she was tall and slender and had green eyes, and had honey-blonde hair that she wore in a neat chignon? It was just the sort of description that Mike O'Donavan would give of her, in his typically uninhibited fashion. She could almost hear him saying it.

Chloe felt herself blushing faintly with annoyance and embarrassment—trust Mike to fill a stranger's head with such nonsense. She said lightly, 'It sounds as if you've been talking to our Dr O'Donavan, Dr Masters. You must take no notice of him and his Irish blarney; he has a vivid imagination.'

'In this case I think that his imagination was within bounds and the description correct,' he said in the same dry tone, his steel-grey eyes surveying her steadily, as if sizing her up. They were, as Susan had said, unnerving.

'Well, let's say that he gets it right occasionally,' Chloe replied, with a rather self-conscious little laugh, cursing herself for feeling ruffled by this rather forbidding and attractive man before her.

'As on this occasion,' he persisted. He gave her one of the smiles that Sue had raved about, and she saw, to her surprise, that his piercing, rather cold grey eyes held for a moment a humorous glint as he looked down at her.

'All right,' she said, deciding to give in graciously. 'Let's say that this time he wasn't so wide of the mark, and you were able to recognise me from his description. But be warned, Dr Masters,' she added with a laugh, 'Mike O'Donavan is a lovely person and a good doctor, but rather over-full of the Gaelic charm. You have to take much of what he says with the proverbial pinch of salt.'

'Really?' he said, one eyebrow raised quizzically, a faint smile still playing round his well-shaped mouth, relaxing his stern features. 'Thanks for the warning,

I'll remember that.' His smile vanished and in an instant he became quite suddenly brisk and professional. 'And now, Sister Lucas, I want to ask you a favour. Will you personally give me a conducted tour of the centre, so that I can refresh my memory and get my bearings before starting work tomorrow? I want to know where everything belongs, and who fits in where. I'd be grateful if you could spare me the time and it is otherwise convenient.'

It was a request, but his cool tone and unsmiling features made it sound more like an order, however politely phrased. She had the impression that here was a man who knew what he wanted, and got it. He would expect her to make time and make it convenient. Well, she couldn't beef about that, it was her job. But she didn't think that she liked him very much in spite of his being a 'handsome hunk', and his occasional smile—there was something too remote and chilling about him.

'Of course, I'll be only too pleased,' she replied with her natural calm, and in her most professional voice. She retrieved her case from the car, closed the windows and locked the door while Dr Masters stood patiently by.

Side by side they walked towards the entrance to the centre, moving out of the shade of the trees into the breathless, unflagging heat of the afternoon sunshine. Chloe glanced surreptitiously at her companion, conscious of his height, and his general air of masculinity and strength. Surprisingly, he still looked cool and composed even in the full glare of the sun, whereas, though she might look as cool as he, she felt anything but composed. Quite the reverse. There was something about this man that made her feel edgy, on guard. Except briefly, when he smiled, his grey eyes gave nothing away; he was polite and superficially pleasant, but she felt that he had depths that she couldn't or wouldn't be allowed to plumb. He looked aloof and distinguished, a secret sort of man who wouldn't welcome intimacy of any sort.

She pushed such ridiculous thoughts out of her head and assumed her role as centre manager. 'This is a good time to look around,' she said, 'as it's pretty quiet. Nearly everyone is out on visits unless they're holding a clinic. Afternoon into evening surgeries go on from four to six. Evening surgeries are from five-thirty to seven, but usually go on till about seven-thirty. Except for the doctors, most of the staff go off duty at six, depending on need. Twice a month there's an evening session for the Well Men and Well Women Clinics from seven till nine. They've really been a success, and are surprisingly well attended. We're all delighted about it.' She glanced at the doctor, whose expression gave nothing away. Was he interested in what she was saying or was he bored? 'But then,' she added apologetically, 'you probably know all this already; you must have heard it at your interview. I'm sorry if I'm overloading you with unnecessary information. I do tend to get carried away when talking about the centre; it's rather a special place to work in. We're a very friendly bunch and believe in teamwork.'

'Well, Sister, I'm looking forward to joining your team, and your enthusiasm does you credit,' he said with quiet sincerity. He turned his head and smiled at her. Her heart skipped a beat. He'd got a lovely mouth when he smiled.

She said a little unevenly. 'Thank you,' and smiled in return.

They were approaching the corner of the building near the entrance when they heard an unseen child's piercing cry. Automatically they quickened their pace and, as they rounded the corner, saw a small boy lying flat on his face on the decorative gravelled area that bordered the path. A heavily pregnant young woman was bending over the child trying to help him up.

'Oh, it's young Jonathan West—trust him to fall over,' said Chloe, hurrying forward. 'His mum's nearly full-term; she'll never manage to get him up.'

In a few easy strides Dr Masters overtook her, reached the child and, firmly moving Mrs West aside, scooped the boy up and set him on his feet. 'Now, then,' he said in a kind, gentle voice, crouching down beside the howling child. 'Stop crying, there's a good lad, and let's see what damage you've done.' Blood was running down one leg. 'Well, you've got a nasty cut on your knee, and your face is a bit grazed just here.' He touched the boy's cheek with infinite gentleness. 'Now have you hurt yourself anywhere else?' His deep voice was very matter-of-fact and reassuring, but full of authority. His smile invited confidence.

To Chloe's and Mrs West's surprise, Jonathan stopped crying, stared at the doctor, whose smiling face was on a level with his, and shook his head. 'No,' he said, sniffing loudly. 'Just my hands are a bit sore, that's all, but it's my leg that really hurts.'

Dr Masters took the child's hands in his and turned them over. The small palms were red and raw where they had scraped along the gravel.

'Nasty,' he said. 'You're being very brave, Jonathan. Look, let's go back inside and get you cleaned up, and bandage that nasty cut on your leg.' He turned to the boy's mother. 'I'm sure your mum thinks that's a good idea, don't you, Mrs West?' he asked.

'Oh, yes, if you think that's what's best. . .' She hesitated for a moment, and then said awkwardly, 'Doctor. . .you are the new doctor, aren't you? I heard you were coming soon.'

'I am. I'm Dr Masters.' He gave the young woman a warm smile, and she blushed with obvious pleasure. He ruffled Jonathan's hair. 'And this young fellow's my first patient at Chidhurst.' He turned to Chloe. 'Now, if Sister will lead the way, we'll get Jonathan sorted out.' He picked the boy up and carried him towards the entrance.

His gesture surprised Chloe—he seemed too formal and austere to pick up a runny-nosed, bloody-kneed little boy.

She was impressed. Well, as long as he's good with the patients, she thought, as she led the little procession through Reception towards the clinic-room, he can be as formal as he likes with me.

Seeing Chloe's surprise because he had picked the boy up, the doctor said softly, 'No point in making the child walk when he's in pain. That's a deep cut that he's got on his knee, with gravel embedded in it. I don't want him to aggravate it.'

'No, of course, and it makes sense to carry him, but I'm afraid your jacket's a casualty too: it's got blood on it.'

If she thought that he would be annoyed about that, she was mistaken. He just shrugged and said mildly, 'Damn, I thought I had avoided that. Never mind, it's par for the course, and with luck it will clean off.'

They reached the well-equipped clinic-room, and

the doctor sat a wide-eyed, scared-looking Jonathan down on the high couch.

'Now, Jonathan,' he explained quietly, 'Sister is going to clean your knee to get off the worst of the dirt, then spray it with something that will help stop the pain, and then I'm going to remove the gravel that's in the cut. Once that's done, we'll put in some antibiotic powder, then stitch you up, and you'll be fine. You'll have a stiff knee for a bit, and you'll have to come back in about five days' time to have your stitches out. But once that's done, you'll be as good as new. Now, do you understand all that?'

Jonathan nodded. 'Yes. But it won't hurt, will it?' he asked tremulously, obviously just holding his tears at bay.

'Hardly at all,' said the doctor truthfully, with a reassuring smile. 'That's what the spray is for. It's called a local anaesthetic, and it takes the feeling out of the skin, so you won't feel me stitching you up. Now, if Sister's ready?' He turned to Chloe.

'Quite ready, Doctor,' she replied, wheeling the dressings trolley she had laid up with all that would be required into position by the couch.

'Good, then let's get on with it,' he said, taking off his jacket and rolling up his shirt sleeves, revealing strong, brown forearms lightly covered with black curling hairs. He went over to the washbasin and scrubbed his hands thoroughly, talking to Jonathan over his shoulder as he did so, constantly reassuring him.

He had lean, long-fingered, competent hands, Chloe noticed, as, after she had cleaned and prepared Jonathan's leg, he began the slow, methodical job of removing minute pieces of gravel from the wound with fine forceps.

It was nearly half an hour later that a cheerful Jonathan, basking in the praise that had been heaped upon him for his bravery, left the clinic-room with his mother. He had a large protective dressing on his knee, and to please him, because he had been so stoical, unnecessary smaller ones on his hands and face.

The clinic-room, thought Chloe, was very peaceful after the Wests had gone, with Jonathan's shrill, rather whiny voice echoing down the corridor as they went. He was not her favourite child. He was generally speaking a spoiled little boy who cried readily, and she was full of admiration for the way that Dr Masters had handled him.

Medically speaking, it had been a simple, if tedious job to pick out the gravel and suture the boy's wound; but the child's personality and an anxious mum could have made it difficult had the doctor not succeeded in getting their co-operation. He was clearly very good with unruly children.

She found herself voicing her thoughts as she tidied up the dressings trolley.

'Yes,' agreed the doctor. 'Children can be difficult little beggars sometimes, but they are our future, and it is up to us to take special care of them. As long as one is honest with them, they seem to be ready to take us on trust, generally speaking. Of course, it doesn't always work, but I do make it a point to explain to children exactly what I am going to do, and not try to fool them. It pays dividends in the end.'

Chloe thought that this sort of speech coming from most people would have sounded pompous and affected, but coming from Dr Masters, in a dry matter-of-fact manner, it sounded like just plain common sense. He was very impressive, and she said in a slightly teasing manner, 'Of course, your special interest is in Paediatrics, isn't it? So I suppose you are rather prejudiced in their favour where children are concerned.' She finished dealing with the trolley and moved to the sink to wash the dishes and instruments that had been used when he'd treated Jonathan.

Head bent over the sink, she didn't see the rather surprised look that passed over his face as she spoke, and was startled when he said in an expressionless voice, 'And you don't care overmuch for children, Sister?'

His remark astonished her. She looked at him sideways, first in amazement and then in anger, quite taken aback by what he had said. Surely she hadn't given the impression that she disliked children? If only he knew how wrong he was. Nothing could be further from the truth. If only he knew how she had longed to have a child, and only fate, or nature, had prevented her. How dared he suggest such a thing?

She turned to face him.

He was standing beside the sink unit, his back to the open window, resting against the worktop, long legs crossed at the ankle, bare brown forearms folded. His well marked brows were drawn together in a frown, above unreadable grey eyes, as he surveyed her down the length of his rather formidable nose. The grey streaks in his thick black hair were silvered in a slanting beam of sunshine. He was, as Sue had said, all man and then some. Chloe was seething with anger, but at the same time was very conscious of his masculinity.

She tore her gaze away from his and back to the sink, scrubbed vigorously at a pair of forceps, and drew in a deep breath to steady herself. 'Of course I care for children, Dr Masters,' she replied in a low, fierce voice. 'I'm surprised that you should think otherwise. I love nursing them. But I like some more than others.' She took in another deep breath. 'And surely that's permissible,' she added sarcastically.

Quite suddenly his cold, distant manner changed, became softer, gentler. 'Of course it is,' he said quietly and, as if realising that he had touched a nerve, continued, 'I'm sorry if I offended you. And you're quite right, it is only natural to prefer some children over others, as long as one doesn't let one's preferences show. But then, you're far too good a nurse to allow that to happen. It was quite obvious when we were dealing with young Jonathan. I had no idea that you even considered him spoilt.'

In the face of his sudden gentleness, and his generous apology, her anger vanished like a burst balloon. 'Thank you,' she said lamely, regretting her earlier sarcasm. 'I'm glad that you can see that I would never let personal feelings interfere with my work. But even you must admit that some children are more appealing than others.'

'Oh, without a doubt, but they are not always the most rewarding to treat, are they? The difficult sort of child offers a challenge, with sometimes remarkable results.'

'Yes, of course that's true, just as it's true of treating adult patients.'

'Absolutely. I'm glad we agree about the basics of good practical medicine.' He gave her a smile which transformed his stern features, and pushed himself away from the worktop as Chloe placed the utensils and instruments that they'd used in the steriliser. He obviously considered the matter closed.

'Now, have you finished in here?' he asked rather abruptly.

'Yes.'

'Then do you think I might still have that conducted tour?'

'Yes, of course, but might I suggest that we go into the staff-room first and have a cup of tea, or a cold drink if you prefer? I don't know about you, but I'm absolutely parched.'

'A cup of tea. What a great idea. Lead the way, Sister.'

The staff-room was empty, and over tea they continued to discuss the day-to-day working of the centre.

Chloe was pleased to have the opportunity to explain some finer points of the nurses' duties at Chidhurst. 'We have here,' she said, 'an unusual situation as regards nursing duties. The practice nurses, employed by the partnership, share some of the visits with the community nurses, who are a bit thin on the ground at present. The Health Authority designates visits for the community nurses and shares their work out with care assistants. This sometimes works well, but in some cases our doctors feel that the patients are not receiving the trained nursing care that they need, and so we take over the borderline patients. So far it's worked, but it takes a great deal of co-operation by all concerned.'

'And that's where you come in, presumably,' said the doctor. 'Deciding who should be seen by trained nurses and who can be left to the attentions of the care assistants.'

'Yes, but my brief goes beyond that. With the approval of the Authority, our practice nurses train some of the care assistants to attend patients with a great deal of expertise. Most of the women practising as assistants are intelligent, caring people, who only need a little guidance to make them expert carers. Given the training and support, they can undertake most practical nursing jobs.'

'It sounds like a very worthwhile effort.'

'Oh, it is. In addition, of course, the practice nurses take some of the strain out of the doctors' lists by doing follow-up visits to patients, where suitable.'

'An ideal arrangement.'

'Well, it seems to work,' said Chloe, swallowing the last of her tea. 'Now, if you are ready, Doctor, shall we start our tour?'

The tour of the centre was a great success. Dr Masters was interested in everything he saw and everyone he met, from the busy pharmacy department to Reception and the staff on duty there. And the interest was reciprocated, thought Chloe wryly, watching her colleagues positively blooming as they responded to the doctor's rather austere charm and rare but attractive smile, as he talked to them about their work.

Their last visit was to the room where the antenatal clinic had been held. There was no one in the waiting area outside, so Chloe tapped casually at the half-open door of the examination-room and entered, to find Alison and Sue, sitting with shoes off and stockinged feet propped on the desk, fanning themselves with patients' notes.

Chloe stopped dead inside the door, and then with

a grin and a muttered apology started to back out. But she had reckoned without the solid form of Dr Masters, who was right behind her. She backed straight into him, and it was clear that he wasn't budging. He looked over Chloe's shoulder and to her surprise, for she wasn't sure how he would react, he gave a muffled chuckle at what he saw.

Alison and Sue seemed mesmerised for a moment, and sat still as statues staring at Chloe and her companion. Then simultaneously they blushed, lowered their feet from the table, and felt around for their errant shoes.

Dr Masters eased past a still-surprised Chloe, and said in his deep voice, 'Please don't move on my account. I'm sure you need to take a break. Very sensible thing to do, elevate your feet and legs.'

Alison groaned as she found her shoes and squashed her feet into them. 'Sorry about this,' she said, pulling a face. 'It's this damned heat, it makes a marathon of all the normal chores, and the antenatal clinic seemed to go on forever.' Belatedly she held out a hand. 'We did meet when you were here last, very briefly. I was called out.'

Ben took her hand. 'I remember. It's nice to meet you again, Dr Knight.' He turned to Sue. 'And it's Sister Ford, isn't it? I met you too, on my last visit.' They shook hands formally, and Sue mumbled a greeting.

She was as near tongue-tied as Chloe had ever seen her, but she was beginning to recover. 'I was just going to fetch a cuppa for Alison and myself,' she said brightly. 'Would you two like one?'

Chloe said quickly, 'No, I won't, thanks, we had some earlier and I must get back to my office. I'm way behind with my work, but Dr Masters may want another cup.'

'Yes, I would, if it's not too much trouble,' he told Sue. 'And perhaps you can fill me in on the antenatal scene,' he said, turning again to Alison. 'I believe I'm taking over from you when you go on leave in a week or so.'

'Indeed you are, for your sins,' said Alison, running a well-shaped hand through her thick, close-cropped, nut-brown hair, widening her hazel eyes and giving him a charming smile.

So he even has you hooked, thought Chloe, watching this little display of femininity from the usually rather cool doctor.

Alison added, 'Be pleased to help. We'll go through the files to put you in the picture, but Sue will be here to put you straight if necessary, won't you, Sue?' she asked.

'If I survive that long in this heat,' said Sue, with an ironic laugh. She seemed to have now recovered her usual sang-froid.

'Well, I'm off,' said Chloe. 'I'll be in my office if you want me, Dr Masters. Don't hesitate to call in if you need anything.'

'Thank you, I'll do that if necessary. And again, my thanks for showing me around and helping me with young Jonathan.'

'A pleasure.' She smiled at him and at Alison, as together she and Sue left the room.

'Isn't he something?' said Sue, as they made their way down the corridor. 'Fancy him remembering me from his last visit. What a dream of a man.'

Privately Chloe thought that it wasn't surprising the new doctor had remembered her friend's brilliant auburn hair and sparkling blue eyes, but all she said was, 'I've got a feeling that our Dr Masters doesn't miss anything much, good or bad. He'll keep us all on our toes.'

'He can use any method he likes to keep me on my toes,' said Sue with a laugh, as they parted at the end of the corridor, she to get tea from the staff-room, and Chloe to make for her office.

Having lost most of the afternoon, Chloe had a mountain of work to get through, and she was still hard at it at six o'clock, when she had hoped to get off duty. She had just decided that she might as well plough on and start the following day with a clear desk when there was a knock at the door. She groaned, and reluctantly called to whoever was knocking to come in. To her surprise, Ben Masters opened the door, and her heart beat a little faster at the sight of him. For some reason, he was the last person she had expected to see; she'd thought that she had done with him for the day.

'Oh,' she said, 'do come in.'

'Are you sure? I can see that you're still up to your eyes in work.'

'There's nothing new about that; half of this job is paperwork.'

'Bureaucracy, the modern disease.'

'Indeed.' He was standing at the other side of the desk, still managing to look cool in his white shirt-sleeves in spite of the thundery heat. 'Oh, please sit down,' she said.

'No,' he said firmly. 'I won't do that, you're too busy. There is something that I want to talk to you about as soon as possible, but it can wait. I'll just say thank you again for looking after me this afternoon.'

'There's no need, it's my job, and anyway, it was a pleasure.'

'Nevertheless, I took up a good deal of your valuable time, and I'm still doing it, so I'll push off and see you in the morning. Goodnight, Sister Lucas.'

'Goodnight, Dr Masters,' she replied with equal formality.

He turned and went out of the room, closing the door quietly behind him.

Chloe stared at the closed door. Why on earth is he so stiff, she wondered, why so formal and reserved? Surely he realised from the way she had made the introductions that nearly everyone was on first-name terms, so why couldn't he relax and be casual? And yet he wasn't uneasy, just deliberately reserved. He was pleasant and polite enough, but for the most part aloof, reticent, almost as if he had something to hide. He was divorced, that much she knew, but surely he wouldn't be secretive about that, would he? Plenty of people were divorced.

She had no answers to any of these questions, and by the time she had finished work she didn't much care. She was hot and tired, and wanted nothing more than a cold shower, a quiet supper, and bed.

It was with relief that she said goodnight to the staff still on duty and let herself out of the centre, and into the car park.

CHAPTER TWO

THE car park was bathed in hazy golden sunshine, but there were large grey clouds piling up on the horizon above the trees, and the air was humid and thundery. Masses of tiny gnats danced in the sunlight, and the scent of lilac from the herbaceous border hung heavy on the air. It looked as if an early summer storm was brewing.

Well, rain would certainly be welcome, thought Chloe, as she drove away from the centre, through the dusty evening traffic of the small town. A little *frisson* of pleasure shot through her, as it always did as she approached the River Chid, which bounded the east side of the town, and home. Home to *Luciana*. *Luciana* was a neatly painted green and white house-boat, one of a dozen boats discreetly moored in the quiet upper reaches of the river. The setting was delightful, lying as it did in the shadow of the beechwood-clad hill, just below the castle.

She arrived at the riverside, and parked her car on the tiny plot of land on the bank that belonged to the houseboat. She sat looking out over the river, and a feeling of intense satisfaction swept over her as she took in the familiar scene. Four years. It didn't seem possible that she had been living on her houseboat for four years. Originally *Luciana* was meant to be a temporary retreat, while she got herself and her affairs sorted out. But life on the river had grown on her and she had been quietly content to stay put, once she had

25

got over the acute shock of Mark's accident and sudden death.

Memories flooded back as she recalled the day that she had moved into *Luciana*. That had been a hot May day too, rather like today, and only weeks after Mark's accident. It had been the fourteenth of May, and her twenty-sixth birthday. She had arrived in Chidhurst, feeling detached, like a zombie, a grieving, withdrawn young widow. Friends had helped her move from her smart London flat. All committed city dwellers, they had been appalled to think that she was prepared to move into this—literally—quiet backwater, even for a few months. 'Stay in town,' they'd said, 'where you know everyone. Start going out and about again. Mark wouldn't want you to shut yourself away like this.'

'You're welcome to stay with me,' her best friend Kate had said, 'until you get yourself sorted out, and get over the worst of the shock.'

It had been impossible to explain that she simply had to make the break with London and her life with Mark, and with their joint friends, while she came to terms with what had happened. Impossible to explain that her grieving was not only for her dead husband, but for what she had discovered the day he died: that he had been having a serious, but discreet, affair with someone else. She had thought their marriage a happy one, one of the few that worked. Only for Mark, apparently, it hadn't been that way. Had he been very unhappy? Had he sought consolation elsewhere because he couldn't find fulfilment with her? She would never know. And she'd never really come to terms with that, since Mark had died.

Mark! Chloe had for the moment a vivid picture of

him, with his fair good looks, his boyish grin. Thank God that they had not managed to conceive the child that she, and she'd thought Mark too, had longed for, in the three years that they had been married. At the time, it had seemed like the one flaw in their marriage, that when they'd started trying for a baby she hadn't readily become pregnant; she had lost some of her usual calm, and had almost panicked at the possibility that she might be infertile.

When a year had passed, she had consulted her doctor, who after discussion and an internal examination had confirmed that there seemed to be no obvious reason why she should not conceive. He advised her to go on trying for a baby normally for another year, before investigating further. 'A year isn't long trying to conceive—some people are simply slow off the mark,' he'd explained. 'There can be all sorts of reasons why you haven't managed it yet, none of them serious or needing outside intervention. But if you don't have any luck within the next year, come back and see me again and we'll start the ball rolling. And before we start investigations on you, which can take some time, we'll do a sperm quality and count on your husband to eliminate him as the reason for your not conceiving.'

And then Mark had died, and it had no longer mattered that perhaps she couldn't bear children; it was purely academic, for she had no intention of marrying ever again. Mark's infidelity had put her off marriage for good.

Well, that was all in her unhappy past. She hadn't thought about Mark clearly in a long while. He was always there of course, deep in her memory, but his image, until now, had faded. Only today, being weatherwise so like the day she had moved on to the river, with the evening sun turning the surface of the water to a molten red-gold, had triggered off sharper memories of the dismal months immediately following Mark's sudden death.

But the months and then the years had passed, and with the help of friendly neighbours and an interesting job she had grown steadily happier. She had begun to live again.

From the start, she had enjoyed her work at the centre, as a member of the close-knit team of doctors and nurses, and when after a couple of years she had been offered the post as centre manager she had felt truly fulfilled and complete.

So much for memories, good and bad; she must put them behind her. The present was what mattered. Resolutely she shook herself out of her reverie and got out of the car. She took a deep breath of fresh riverside air, and with a sigh of satisfaction went on board the houseboat.

She stood for a moment on the side deck, looking round with intense pleasure at the tubs of flowers and shrubs that decorated the fore and aft decks, standing sentinel on either side of the short gangplank which connected the boat to the shore. They would want watering later on when it got a bit cooler. Unlocking the white-painted front door which sported a fish-tail brass knocker, she let herself into the spacious open-plan cabin, with its comfortable sitting and dining areas and a galley of a kitchen.

Usually she stopped off in the day cabin to have a drink and read her mail, but tonight she went straight through to the bathroom, *en suite* with her bedroom, intent on having the shower to which she had been looking forward all afternoon. Her drink and post could wait.

Vague memories lingered and exercised her mind as she slipped out of her clothes and turned on the shower. The water was tepid in the cold tap, but refreshing enough on her hot skin. She unpinned her honey-blonde hair and shampooed it, revelling in the cool water washing the scented bubbles from each long strand.

Slowly she started to relax, and her mind, after its former activity, began to blank out her disturbing thoughts. By the time she had finished showering, Mark's ghost no longer filled her mind. He had receded again into the shadows of the past.

But oddly, as she was drying and powdering herself, the image of another man replaced it. Dr Masters was suddenly there, sharply in focus, with his well-cut, thick, grey-streaked hair, commanding features and piercing grey eyes. Unbidden came the picture of him crouching beside the small, injured boy, Jonathan West, gently comforting and reassuring him. Such a large man, to be so gentle.

Now why on earth had he come into her mind? She was totally surprised by this unexpected image. She hadn't consciously been thinking about him, so why had this stranger suddenly invaded her space?

With an effort she pushed the vision aside. So much for Dr Ben Masters!

She changed into cool, white silk pyjamas, and went through to her neat little galley, poured herself a glass of ice-cold white wine, and prepared a tuna salad, which she took up to the sun deck to eat. It was sheer bliss to sit high above the river on the railed-in flat roof of the cabin, and sip at her wine and eat her supper.

The ominous clouds of early evening had disappeared, but there had been rumbles of thunder in the distance, and somewhere not too far away there had been a storm which had freshened the air. The golden evening sunshine gleamed and shimmered on the still waters. An occasional boat was sailed or rowed upriver, an occasional fish leapt out of the water and fell back with a soft plop. A few walkers strolled along the towpath, making for the riverside pub half a mile downstream. Children's faint disembodied voices rang out from the tree-sheltered gardens that backed on to the towpath. And poised over all, silhouetted against the sky-line on top of the hill, towering protectively, rose the castellated mass of Chidhurst Castle.

All together, it was a perfect evening, and a perfect end to a busy and somewhat disturbing day, Chloe thought. Disturbing, because the new doctor had made his unexpected appearance, and had made, whether she liked it or not, an impact on her.

In spite of his, at times, distant manner, she felt in her bones that Ben Masters was going to be right for Chidhurst, though he might take some getting used to. He didn't seem like an easy man to get to know, and on a personal level she didn't much care for him. But, whatever his personal hang-ups, she was sure that he would be a caring and clever doctor, and her beloved centre would be well served by him. At the end of the day that was all that mattered.

The heat and the wine made her drowsy and she decided on an early night. She watered her plants, and went to bed just as a purple dusk descended and the sun set in all its multicoloured glory behind the castle.

Her thoughts were still with the health centre and the enigmatic, and at the same time charismatic, Ben Masters.

She lay awake for a long time, going over the events of the day, until, at last, lulled by the faint slap of the water against the hull, she fell into a dreamless sleep.

May turned into June, and the weather remained hot. Summer colds, hay fever, sunburn and stings had taken over from bronchitis, hypothermia and other typical winter ills. The waiting area in the health centre always seemed to be full of short-term visiting patients as well as the regulars and, with various members of staff on holiday, those left on duty were working flat-out.

It was about ten days after his arrival at the centre that Ben Masters, who had taken over Alison Knight's patients while she was away, appeared in Chloe's office during morning surgery hours.

He looked as he always did, cool and immaculate, in well-tailored, conventionally correct clothes. Today he was wearing dark blue cotton trousers, pale blue silk shirt, and a blue and silver striped tie. The blue seemed to give depth and warmth to his steely grey eyes, which were focused upon her.

He and Chloe had both been so busy since he had started work at the centre that, except for passing the time of day, she had seen very little of him. To her surprise, his appearance in her room gave her a jolt of unexpected pleasure. He looked incredibly masculine and solid and utterly reliable as he stood in her doorway. Her breathing quickened.

'Good morning, might I have a word?' he asked.

'Of course, what can I do for you?' she replied brightly, relieved that her voice came out evenly.

'Well, I'm hoping you can enlighten me. Just what does the cryptic message, "See manager before treating" mean, written at the bottom of this patient's current notes?' He pulled a card from the familiar buff envelope containing a patient's medical records.

'I've no idea. May I see?' She held out a hand for the card.

'Certainly.' He handed over both card and file.

Chloe read the name on the envelope. 'Oh,' she said softly. 'It's poor Janice Moorland.'

'Poor Janice Moorland!' he repeated. 'Well, can you enlighten me?'

'Of course. This is connected with an incident that occurred some time ago. Something that could happen in any practice. Janice is very impressionable and tends to get crushes on her doctors. A while ago she went a bit further than having a crush, and quite seriously made up to one of our learner GPs when he was examining her. He told her to stop her nonsense; she threatened to say that he'd made advances to her. Adrian, the young doctor in question, acted quickly. He hauled in a passing nurse and told her in front of the patient exactly what had happened, then repeated the story with a couple of senior colleagues present, until Janice agreed that his was a true version of events. She was told that in future she would be seen by a female doctor or, if seen by a male doctor, she would be chaperoned. She's not been any trouble since, nor likely to be, I think. She frightened herself as much as our doctor, but obviously Alison wanted you put in the picture, should you have to see her. I expect she meant to mention it to you before going on leave.'

'Well, she didn't. But I'm glad she wrote this note. Thanks for filling me in. I've got Miss Moorland in my consulting-room at this moment, complaining of general abdominal pain and dysmenorrhoea, though she's not very clear whether her worst pain occurs when she has a period or not. I'll have to examine her. Can you loan me a nurse to chaperon, please?'

'I'll come myself. Everyone else is busy.'

He raised an eyebrow and waved a hand over her paper-laden desk. 'And you're not,' he said ironically.

Chloe laughed. 'Papers can wait, people can't,' she said crisply.

'How refreshing to find a manager who understands that.'

'I spent long enough on the other side of the fence to know where the priorities lie, and I still manage to do a bit of hands-on nursing.'

'So I see.'

As they made for his room, Chloe caught a whiff of his cologne, and was very aware of his powerful presence as he strode beside her. His arm touched hers, and she was conscious of short, wiry black hairs on strong forearms, brushing feather-light against her bare skin. It was like a tiny electric shock. Automatically she moved sideways out of touching range.

'Do you want me to come in straight away, or do you want to talk to Janice first?' she asked, as they reached the door.

'Oh, come in immediately, please.' He gave a wry smile, and in a rather caustic tone added, 'Don't leave me at the mercy of our Miss Moorland. I know it's not likely, but she may try to take advantage of me as I'm new. One can never tell, and I've absolutely no intention of taking any chances.'

Chloe was surprised by his forcefulness. Surely he was too mature and experienced to be bothered by the situation? But however forceful he was when talking to her, he was very gentle when talking to his patient.

'Do you mind,' he asked Janice, in a kindly, matter-of-fact voice, 'if Sister is in the room while I examine you?'

Janice shook her head. 'No, I don't mind,' she said listlessly. 'As long as you can find out what's wrong with me, I don't care. I'm fed up with having this pain all the time. I should have come before, but I thought it would go away. I just want you to do something about it.'

There is no doubt, thought Chloe, that Janice really is having problems this time. She isn't play-acting or trying to attract the doctor's attention. Her usually pretty curly hair looked greasy and neglected, and her make-up carelessly applied.

Ben obviously thought that she was genuine too, for he started to question her in a quiet, encouraging voice. 'Have you only started to have really painful periods recently?'

Janice nodded. 'Yes, last month and again this month, and in between I've had this sort of dull ache in my tummy, down here.' She pointed to her lower abdomen. 'It just won't go away at all.' Her cornflower-blue eyes filled with tears. 'And I feel sick sometimes, and, well, just generally not very well.'

'And you're not menstruating at this moment, and you've still got the pain?'

Janice nodded.

'Right then, Miss Moorland, I'd better examine you and see if we can find out what's wrong. Will you hop up on the couch behind the curtain, please? Sister will give you a hand to get your things off. I want to have a look at your tummy and probably do an internal examination too.' He gave her a nice smile, and turned back to his desk.

Chloe helped Janice remove her skirt and panties and covered her with cotton blankets, leaving just the area from waist to hip exposed.

She announced that they were ready, and Ben started his external examination. Gently he palpated and pressed the young woman's abdomen, looking for signs of rigidity or guarding, to give him a clue as to what was wrong. Janice winced and drew in her breath sharply as he worked his way down her side, and she repeated the sharp intake of breath when he slipped one hand beneath her back and pressed down with the other.

He straightened up and said, 'Now I'm going to have a look inside, Miss Moorland. Just draw up your knees please and open them.' Janice did as he asked, and Chloe draped the blanket tent-like over her knees. He went on to explain, 'The instrument I'm going to use may feel a little cold and uncomfortable, but it shouldn't hurt. It will hold back the vagina walls so that I can see what's going on in there. Do you understand what I am going to do?'

'Yes.'

'Good, this won't take long.'

Chloe, anticipating his needs, handed him the speculum from the permanently laid-up trolley at the foot of the couch. He took the instrument from her and nodded his thanks and then carefully, with practised fingers, inserted it into Janice's vagina, and began his internal examination.

'Right,' he said after a few minutes, removing the speculum, 'that's all done; you can get dressed now.'

He moved away and wrote up the treatment card while he was waiting. 'Now,' he said, when Janice was sitting in the chair by his desk, 'I don't think you have anything to worry about. You seem to have a small ovarian cyst which is causing your pain and feeling of nausea and giving you a bit of a temperature. The best treatment for this is a painkiller and an antibiotic, which I will prescribe, and warmth and bed rest for a few days. I think you'll find then that your symptoms will subside, and you'll feel much better in a week or so. If the pain persists, or returns, you must come back to see me and I'll refer you to hospital for further investigation.'

'A cyst? That's not like cancer, is it?' she asked fearfully.

'No, not the simple cyst that I believe you have. It can easily be treated in the way that I've suggested, and there's nothing for you to worry about. Is there anybody at home who will look after you while you rest?'

'Oh, yes, my mother's there, she'll love looking after me.'

'Good, you can't beat mother-love,' said Ben with a smile as he handed her her prescription. 'Get that filled at the pharmacy, and then home and bed. You need a couple of weeks off work, perhaps longer if the cyst's stubborn, as they sometimes can be. Do you want a sick certificate for your employer?'

Janice nodded. 'Yes, please.' Ben wrote out the certificate and handed it to her. 'Thank you very much, Doctor,' she said, sounding pathetically grateful. 'And you too, Sister. Thank you for being so nice.' She gave them both a small, wan smile as she left the consulting-room.

'Poor girl,' said Ben. 'She's obviously very conscious of how she behaved in the past, and is regretting it. One can't help feeling sorry for her, though she might have caused irreparable damage to your young GP.'

'Yes, I think we were concerned about him. He was so vulnerable, being new and untried.'

'Well, age and reputation are not necessarily proof against such accusations in our line of business. One is repeatedly at risk from certain females. We always need to be on our guard.'

Chloe said quietly, 'That's true, all medical people are vulnerable by the very nature of their work. But thank goodness most patients, including women, want to form a friendly rapport with their doctor and nothing more. And I think that they appreciate their doctor being straight with them, but expect a degree of gentleness and understanding regarding problems other than their immediate health. They like their GP to be interested in them as people as well as patients.'

Ben gave her a rather grim little smile that quirked the corners of his mouth but didn't reach his eyes. Chloe was reminded of what Sue had said about him being world-weary. That's how he looked now. As if he'd heard it all before, and didn't believe it. 'You're talking about caring for the whole person and not just the sick bit, aren't you?' he said drily. 'Very commendable. In a perfect world, all doctors would like to do that, but with time the enemy it's not always practical, I'm afraid. One does one's best, of course, but at the end of the day it's a question of getting through a list of patients and treating their medical problems.'

His piercing eyes met hers for a moment, their grey depths unreadable. He looked down at his slim gold wristwatch, and said crisply, 'Which reminds me, Sister, I'd better get on and finish these notes. I've no one else to see here, but I've a long list of patients to visit.' He sat down at his desk.

Chloe said flatly, feeling deflated by his almost cynical remarks about not getting involved with patients' private lives, 'Yes, I've got to get on too, but I'll just sort this out first.' She turned to the trolley and the rumpled couch. Her thoughts raced as she neatly folded the blankets, and put a clean paper strip on the couch.

What a strange man he was, so obviously kind and understanding with people when they were ill, and yet lukewarm when she spoke about patient involvement. Surely he wanted to form a rapport with his patients, adults as well as children. Unless, of course, he was simply hiding his essential kindness under a veneer of cynicism. She hoped this was the case, otherwise he would always be something of an outsider. What a pity if he had brought his big city ideas with him, and was going to be forever a stranger in the friendlier ambience of a small-town practice.

She finished tidying up. 'Well, I must be off,' she said to his broad back as he sat busily writing at his desk. 'I'll take these with me and pop them into the steriliser in the clinic room as I go,' she added, picking up the speculum and other items that he had used in his examination.

He stood up and turned round. 'Thank you, that's

kind of you. And thanks for your help with Miss Moorland.'

'Think nothing of it.' She felt as stiff and formal as he sounded.

She put out a hand to open the door, but he reached it first and opened it for her. Coolly, she nodded her thanks.

To her astonishment he said, as she stepped into the corridor, 'You made an interesting point about patient care. I'd like to hear more. Maybe we can fix something when we are off duty—a meal perhaps. . . Meanwhile there's something else I've been wanting to discuss with you, as manager, since I first arrived. I've just been so damned busy, I haven't had a chance. If you're in your office later this afternoon, perhaps we might have a word?'

Chloe gathered herself together. 'Isn't it your half-day?' she asked.

'Yes, but I'm most anxious to talk to you about a project that I have in mind. A half-day is a small sacrifice to make.'

'I'll be free after four.'

'I'll see you then.'

'Right.' She nodded. 'See you at four.'

Their eyes caught and held for a second or so, and then she walked away. There was an expression in his that she couldn't fathom; they were not their usual steely, piercing grey, but warmer, softer. She breathed in deeply once her back was to the man. He mustn't know or guess that she felt peculiarly uplifted by their eye-contact. Had he been affected by it too? she wondered.

* * *

Chloe returned to her office after dropping off in the clinic-room the instruments that needed sterilising, her mind in a whirl. Ben Masters had seemed his usual reserved self at first as they worked together, and had given a very cool reception to her well-intentioned suggestions for closer ties with his patients; but suddenly he had softened. He had intimated that he wanted to know more about her ideas, and had even hinted at taking her out for a meal to talk about her theories. And he was prepared to give up his own precious time off to discuss some project of his own connected with his work. The man was certainly a fascinating enigma, protective of his privacy yet showing signs of being ready to listen to an informed viewpoint.

With a shrug of impatience she put aside her turbulent thoughts of the doctor, and sat down at her desk to attack her paperwork. She had been hard at it for some time when the phone rang, and Betty Box's voice said in her ear, 'I've got Joy Nicolas's husband on the line—will you have a word?'

'Yes, of course,' she said cheerfully, though her heart sank. Joy was her second-in-command, a super nurse, and this afternoon in an on-call and treatment role. She would have a dozen or more patients booked for ear syringing, removal of stitches and antihistamine jabs, as well as a host of other jobs. If her husband Andy was phoning it could only mean that Joy was sick and couldn't come on duty, and she herself would have to take over Joy's duties. That meant another afternoon's paperwork put aside, and no meeting with Ben Masters at four. She wouldn't be free until at least five, perhaps later. Pity; she had been looking forward to her meeting with him. She squashed her disappointment.

Joy had a migraine, to which she was occasionally subject. Chloe metaphorically rolled up her sleeves and prepared for her stint in the clinic-room that afternoon. Her meeting with Ben was off. She rang Reception and asked to be informed when he arrived back from his visits.

She settled down to tackle her admin. work, and phoned through a large order to the wholesale suppliers for syringes, needles and specimen bottles and other items needed for the clinic-room. By the time she had entered the order into her stock-book and filled in the complicated analysis sheet to keep a check on goods used by the ever-increasing practice, it was twelve-thirty.

Betty rang through to say that she was closing Reception and going off for lunch, and Dr Masters had not yet returned from his visits.

Chloe reassured her. 'Not to worry, Betty, I'm having sandwiches in my office while I wrestle with next week's duty roster—and you know what that's like.'

'I certainly do, you poor old thing—what a way to spend your lunch hour. By the way, you won't forget that Marjory will be off, will you?'

'No, I've got her request; I'll make sure her times are covered. Sonia's offered to do some extra duties, so you should be OK. It's when people don't give fair warning of wanting time off that I really tear my hair out, especially if I've just completed the chart.'

'I can imagine. Anyway, we're away now, and everyone else has gone. See you this afternoon.'

'See you.'

Silence, except for a fly buzzing at the sun-filled window, settled over Chloe's office and the rest of the centre. The silence was all the more pronounced because the building was normally a noisy hive of activity, with a full waiting-room, and doctors, nurses and receptionists going about their business.

Chloe rather liked the quiet and the emptiness. She kicked off her shoes and wriggled her toes appreciatively. While there was no one about, she could wander around in her stockinged feet. A wonderful feeling of freedom and pride engulfed her as she meandered about the empty building. The centre was her own little kingdom, her responsibility. It was hard but rewarding work, and it encroached on her free time, but she loved it. It was her job to see that everything ran smoothly. Here she felt in control, of herself as well as the staff, and she had needed to feel in control ever since she had discovered Mark's infidelity. She needed, for her peace of mind, to know what she was doing and where she was heading, and here she had found it. Nothing and no one was going to spoil that for her, she thought fiercely. She was astonished by her own fierceness. Why was she feeling so defensive? Her position wasn't being threatened.

The silence, and her errant and unexpected thoughts, were broken by the sound of the double locks being turned on the front door.

Ben Masters! Damn, he would come now. Hastily she swallowed a mouthful of egg and cress sandwich, and hurried along the corridor to the sanctuary of her office. She had no wish to meet him bare-foot, and with a mouthful of food.

She would go and see him once she had tidied up.

She retrieved her shoes, tidied her hair, renewed her make-up, and made her way back along the corridor.

The door of his room was ajar. She tapped at it softly, and smiled to herself as she heard a smothered exclamation from within. She had evidently taken him by surprise. Clearly he wasn't expecting anyone else to be in the building.

His deep voice invited her to enter.

He was seated at his desk, busily writing. He stopped and looked up as she entered. For the briefest of moments a surprised, but clearly pleased, expression flitted across his face. His eyes lit up with unusual warmth as they met hers. All the steel had gone out of them, leaving them a misty blue-gey. He stood up quickly. His eyes continued to hold hers. 'Oh,' he said softly, 'Chloe, it's you. What are you doing here? It's lunch-time.'

He'd actually used her Christian name! How surprising and refreshing to find that he was capable of unbending. She felt curiously touched. 'I brought sandwiches, knowing that I was going to be busy, even barring emergencies,' she explained, all at once feeling strangely detached, and conscious that the centre was empty and deathly quiet. It was as if the two of them were alone in the world. What a ridiculous thought to have in the middle of the day. Most peculiar.

'You work too hard,' he said in his deep, velvet voice, his eyes still locked on hers.

'It goes with the job, and I don't mind, I love my work,' she said breathlessly. Her normal voice seemed to have deserted her. The feeling of unreality persisted.

'That's obvious,' he said drily. 'No one could doubt your single-mindedness.' For a moment longer they stared silently at each other, then he waved to the chair by his desk. 'Please sit down,' he said softly.

His eyes left hers, and Chloe felt for a moment as if she were suspended in mid-air, an extraordinary sensation. Then common sense returned and she gathered herself together. 'No, I won't sit, thanks,' she said coolly. 'I simply haven't the time. I just came to tell you that our meeting at four is off. I've got to fill in for someone who has gone sick. I'm sorry about that.'

'So am I. I was looking forward to putting you in the picture about my idea.'

'Well, at least you will have your half-day free.'

He made a disparaging gesture with his hand. 'That matters not a jot,' he said impatiently. 'I would much rather have talked about this project. I suppose it will be too late to have a word when you finish this evening; you'll want to get off home.' It was half a question, half a statement, and he added, 'I could offer you a reasonable meal at the Castle Arms, my home from home at the moment, until I find permanent accommodation. As it's virtually your local, you must know that the food there is very good—plain but well cooked.'

'Are you trying to tempt me, Dr Masters?' she asked huskily, with a little laugh.

'In a word, yes.' He could see that she was wavering. 'Shall we say seven-thirty?'

'Let's say eight o'clock; that will give me plenty of time to get home and change.'

'Fine, I'll pick you up.'

'No, thanks, there's no need. I'd rather come under my own steam.' She had no desire to be closeted in a car with this austere, clever man, trying to make small talk.

'Are you sure?'

'Positive. Anyway, the Arms is not far from me. I might even walk.'

'Well, at least if you do you won't have a drink-drive problem, and I shall be able to ply and bribe you with strong liquor,' he said to her surprise, and a broad, quirky smile hovered round his well-shaped mouth, suddenly making him look younger.

Chloe laughed in response to this frivolous nonsense. 'Well, bribery will get you nowhere, Dr Masters,' she said cheerfully. 'But you can always try.'

'I'll do just that, Sister Lucas, and I warn you, I'm pretty determined. I'm quite prepared to do battle to get my own way.'

'Then let battle commence at eight this evening,' she said, moving towards the door.

His smile broadened and his steely grey eyes gleamed with sudden humour. 'Once more unto the breach,' he said, and held the door open for her.

She brushed against him as she moved into the corridor, and, just as she had earlier that morning, she caught the faintest whiff of expensive aftershave.

'Goodbye,' she murmured, as she walked away from him.

'*Au revoir*,' he said. 'Till eight.'

For the second time that day, he watched her with admiration as she walked down the long corridor.

CHAPTER THREE

CHLOE walked to the Castle Arms through the hazy early evening sunshine, feeling somewhat apprehensive about having dinner with Ben Masters. He was still, after a fortnight at Chidhurst, an unknown quantity. He remained, except with the children, with whom he had a remarkable rapport, polite, but detached and impersonal. She was by no means sure that she even liked the man, though in a peculiar sense she felt drawn to him by some strange kind of chemistry. Today there had been a bit of a breakthrough when they'd had snatches of thoughtful conversation, and exchanged searching looks. And then this unexpected invitation.

Perhaps he was beginning to thaw, and the evening would turn out to be sociable and relaxed. Of course, from his point of view it was to be a working dinner, a means to an end, she reminded herself. But in spite of being aware of this, and her reservations about him, she couldn't prevent a little thrill of excitement coursing through her as she anticipated dining with the enigmatic doctor. Sue and the others at the centre would envy her this evening, for in varying degrees they were all intrigued by the remote and aloof Ben Masters and would have jumped at the chance of getting to know him better.

He was waiting for her on the small flagged and railed terrace of the hotel overlooking the High Street, and she saw him as she mounted the steps of the terrace. He came forward to meet her, hand outstretched.

'Hello there.' He smiled a greeting that lit up his chiselled features.

'Good evening.' She smiled in return.

'May I suggest that we sit out here and have a drink before we go in to dinner?' he said, steering her towards one of the tables, shaded by a brightly striped umbrella. 'I'm sure you could do with something long and cool after your walk.'

'I certainly could. A white wine spritzer with ice would be wonderful.'

He settled her in a chair. 'I'll not be long.'

He disappeared into the dim interior of the ancient hostelry that nestled against the massive wall surrounding the castle grounds, to fetch their drinks.

A quite unexpected feeling of proprietorial pleasure swept over her as she noted the admiring glances he received from several other women on the terrace. As always, he was looking handsome and distinguished, his grey-streaked black hair and strong features enhanced by the pale grey, beautifully tailored suit, white silk shirt, and muted but colourful tie that he was wearing. The well-cut suit emphasised his broad shoulders and narrow hips, making him look very fit, very masculine, Chloe thought, as he strode away.

She was glad that she had taken time and trouble choosing what to wear. She knew that she looked good, a match for any man however well groomed. Her lightweight, straw-coloured, short-skirted suit teamed perfectly with a wild silk blouse of green and gold, which glowed jewel-like in the evening sunlight. Small green stud earrings emphasised the green of her eyes, and a smooth chignon hairdo completed the overall effect of casual elegance that she had aimed for.

Instinct had told her to present the right image to Ben Masters, the image of a professional woman enjoying a social-cum-working occasion with a colleague, and nothing on a more personal level. No way did she intend to invade his privacy, and she wanted him to be aware of this.

Deep in thought, she didn't notice Ben returning with their drinks until he placed in front of her a tall frosted glass with ice clinking in it invitingly.

'Our table in the restaurant will be ready in about ten minutes,' he said. 'I brought the menus with me so that we can take our time choosing what we want.' He handed her a menu card and took his seat opposite her. He looked composed and remote as he picked up his glass and took a long drink.

Chloe sighed inwardly. She wished that he would unbend a little; he sounded so formal. It didn't augur well for the evening if he was going to keep up this excessive correctness. She took a sip of her drink. 'Lovely,' she said politely, and equally formally. 'Thank you.'

It must be catching, she thought, and wished that she could think of something bright and funny to say, but her mind was a blank. She began studying the lengthy menu. 'Is there anything you can suggest,' she asked, 'as you're in residence, as it were, and must be familiar with most of the dishes? It's ages since I was here for a meal.'

'Well, for starters I can certainly recommend the cold cream of cucumber soup. It's delicious, and just right on a night like this.'

'And as a main course?'

'Any one of the fish dishes, or saddle of lamb and redcurrant jelly, or chicken Florentine, which is prepared with various herbs and spinach and cheese, and baked in a sauce. It's quite an experience, and one of the few fancy dishes that they do here.'

'Well, you've sold me on the cucumber soup and the chicken Florentine. What about a pudding?'

'It has to be the fresh rhubarb tart and cream; it's mouthwatering.'

'Right, I'll put myself in your hands, and be guided entirely by you.'

'Really?' His eyes actually twinkled at the unintended innuendo. 'You could do worse.'

'Oh, I'm sure I could,' replied Chloe with a laugh.

This little play on words eased the tension, and from then on the evening, after the shaky start, began to improve.

They stayed on the terrace and, surprisingly, chatted easily about all manner of things until they were called to their table. The aloof Dr Masters had certainly begun to unbend. Chloe wondered if the evening might after all turn out to be more social than work-orientated, but it was soon obvious that this was not to be.

'Now, are you ready to hear about my project?' he asked as soon as they were seated in the restaurant. It was a window table, overlooking the uneven, jumbled rooftops of the town, which appeared to be tumbling down the steep hillside to the river. A lovely view, with the myriad tiled rooves bathed orange-red in the late evening sunshine.

Chloe turned her head from the window and gave him a smile, which hid her disappointment. So the rest of the evening was to be work; they'd had their bit of socialising, and that was that. And she still knew very little about the man; their conversation on the terrace had been interesting but quite impersonal. 'That's what I'm here for, Dr Masters, to discuss your project,' she said stiffly.

He surprised her by saying, 'Ben, please. After all, we are off duty.'

Her heart surged with pleasure at his suggestion. Was this at last a really friendly signal?

'That's what I'm here for, Ben,' she repeated with a little teasing laugh, thrilled with the small breakthrough in his reserve. 'I'm earning my dinner.'

He smiled broadly in return, appreciating her teasing. 'So you are,' he said. 'Splendid, then if you don't mind talking about this while we eat. . .?' He paused, a question mark in his voice.

'Not at all. I expected to do just that.'

'Good—well, the position is this. With your help, and my colleagues' support, I want to start a teenagers' health club.'

'A teenagers' health club!' she repeated in a surprised voice. 'I'm sorry, I must be dense. I'm not with you.'

'Well, we have our successful baby, infant and adult clinics, but there's a gap in the market. The thirteen to sixteen-year-olds have no special care facilities of their own, no real equivalent to these "well" clinics at their local surgery.'

'But do they need it? Surely they're taken care of at school, with their biology and hygiene lessons?'

'Yes, they're well instructed, but I'd like to offer help and advice on a more individual basis. I'd like to complement the good job that the schools are doing. Young people are very receptive at that age, if you can capture their imagination. If we could hammer home messages about how to keep fit, and why they should, it's possible that *some* of them might be prevented from picking up bad or dangerous habits.'

'You mean like experimenting with drugs?'

'Among other things. But generally teach them good habits for a lifetime—about sensible diet and exercise, for instance. Not all parents have got the message yet that it's something one should start early in life. It's a waste not to try.'

His chiselled face was alight with enthusiasm, and his grey eyes were softer, warmer, as he leant forward and talked animatedly about a subject that was obviously near to his heart. Chloe felt herself warming to the man and the doctor; his enthusiasm was infectious.

The waiter arrived with their chicken Florentine.

When they were alone again Chloe said, picking her words carefully, not wanting to sound too dampening but seeing all sorts of problems ahead, 'Well, it's quite a revolutionary idea, but a lot of people will take convincing, and we'll have to take care not to tread on people's toes. The schools may look on it as a criticism of their teaching and the parents might feel that their authority is threatened.'

'Well, that's the last thing I intend. After all, no one would be forced to join the club. All I want to do is provide a listening and advice service. Some parents may even welcome the support, since teenagers are notoriously difficult to deal with. As for revolutionary, so were the Well Woman clinics when they were first started—now they're commonplace.'

'Do you know of any other doctors who operate similar schemes for young people?'

'No, not offhand, but I believe some social services are trying to put something like it into practice.' He paused and, laying down his knife and fork, leaned slightly across the table, compelling her to look at him. He said, in a low, intense voice, 'Chloe, think about the youngsters we might help who are desperately worried about being too fat, or too thin, too short or too tall. Think how they worry about the odd spot or greasy hair. Life can be hell at that age. Think what a relief it would be for them to be able to talk to someone about their problems, someone who cares and can sympathise, but who isn't too close to them.'

'And you think that we could provide that sort of service?'

'I think we should try. Give them a healthy living programme to follow, listen to their woes. Help them through this difficult period in their lives. It's a long-term project, of course, but for some of these young people we may provide a lifeline right now. It's worth considering, isn't it?' he asked softly.

Her eyes met his, and she saw a wealth of gentleness and compassion mirrored in them.

She said softly, 'You've come up against something in the past which makes you feel strongly about this, haven't you, Ben?'

He stared at her in silence for a moment, and then said quietly, 'Yes. A girl of thirteen, overweight and dreadfully unhappy, only none of us realised it until she took an overdose of her mother's sleeping tablets. Oh, she survived, just, but no thanks to the adults around her who wouldn't take her misery seriously. Nobody appreciated what she was going through. In some cases this could be why bulimia and anorexia nervosa and other problems start—because adults won't take a child's unhappiness seriously. That's what young people want, to be taken seriously. Who knows what problems we may avert if we do? And think what a help and support we could be to the parents. They're often as much at sea as the child.'

'It'll be a big undertaking. We have to set aside a room, say once or twice a month, for the club meeting. And you will need a nurse to assist. That means extra duty or overtime for nursing help. It won't be cheap to run, supposing it gets off the ground. And to do that it will need publicity. Leaflets to all patients, notices in the surgery. And to keep local goodwill we'll have to talk to the schools and let them know what we plan to do. And it'll need costing out before we go any further.'

'I understand that, which is why I've come to you first before trying to interest anyone else.'

At this point a waiter appeared to remove their plates, and another to set their puddings in front of them. To Chloe's surprise, she realised that she had finished her chicken Florentine almost without tasting it, so absorbed had she been in their conversation.

She said quietly, 'Well, you've given me an awful lot to think about. Leave it with me for a while to mull over. It's an exciting concept, and one that I think will command a lot of sympathy, but I need to come up with something more concrete before putting it to a senior staff meeting.'

Ben sat back in his chair, relaxed and smiling. 'I understand,' he said. 'And I'm happy to leave it in your hands. I'm sorry I've mucked up most of your meal. Now, do enjoy your pudding, I promise I won't say another word about the project. Let your taste buds get to work on the rhubarb tart.'

'I'd appreciate that,' she said with a little laugh, as she dug her fork into the fabulously light pastry, determined to concentrate on her food and close her senses to his hypnotic presence.

They carried on a casual and, thanks to Ben's dry humour, amusing conversation as they ate their pudding. When they finished, they opted to have their coffee and brandy on the now softly lit terrace. Dusk was falling, and lights were twinkling in latticed windows all over the old town. The lights in the high street came on and cascaded down the steep hill like an amber necklace. The castle on top of the hill sprang to life, illuminated by concealed beams of rosy light. It was all incredibly romantic.

'Chidhurst at its best,' murmured Chloe.

'I'm hooked on it already,' said Ben softly. 'What a town to work and live in—and I shall enjoy it even more when I've found a place of my own.'

'Oh, so you'll be house-hunting, then.' Chloe almost held her breath. At last something personal.

'I've already begun. I've looked at a couple of places, but they were no good. I've got a few more to look at over the next week or so. The trouble is that properties for sale in Chidhurst are not thick on the ground, although there are plenty outside the town itself.'

'That's true; it's because the old town is so compact, with the river on one side and the hill and the castle grounds on the other. There's no room for new building, so it's just a question of old properties changing hands, which they don't do that often. People tend to come here and stay here, and some are lucky enough to be born here.'

'You seem very attached to the place. Were *you* born here?'

'No, I moved here four years ago, and now I wouldn't live anywhere else.'

'You've no ambitions to move on, perhaps to manage a larger practice?'

'None whatsoever. The Chidhurst practice is quite large enough and presents me with plenty of challenges, such as the one you've thrown at me tonight,' she said with a laugh. 'And the practice will probably extend further to cater for the new estates being built outside the town. Thank goodness we've enough room within the centre grounds to build on extra surgeries, if they are needed in the future.'

A warm, humid darkness fell as they talked, and they hardly noticed, but a rumble of thunder in the distance brought Chloe suddenly to her feet. 'Good lord, I must go,' she said. 'It sounds as if there might be a storm brewing, and by the time I get home it'll be after eleven.' She unhooked her bag from the chair.

'Do you mean to walk?'

'Yes, if I can beat the storm.'

'You're not walking at this time of night, at least not on your own,' said Ben firmly. 'It's either a taxi or you let me escort you.' His grey eyes, gleaming in the soft terrace light, caught and held hers for a moment. 'I mean it,' he added. 'Even Chidhurst is no place for a woman to wander in after dark.'

There was another rumble of thunder, and distant flashes of lightning, heralding a typical summer storm.

Chloe did a quick think about whether to accept his offer to escort her, or take a taxi. She was touched by his thoughtfulness. He was obviously genuinely concerned for her safety. Of course, he couldn't know that she had walked around in Chidhurst many times after dark, and was not in the least nervous. If he insisted on escorting her, would it spoil the evening, which had turned out better than she had expected? Ben had thawed considerably towards the end, although she had still learned precious little about him. But if he walked home with her she would have to invite him in for coffee, and some sixth sense warned her that they were not yet ready for a *tête-à-tête* over the coffee-cups in her little galley. The evening would perhaps drag to an untidy finish, stretching to the limits the tenuous threads of friendship that had begun to form between them. And that wouldn't do—much better to finish the evening cleanly.

'It had better be a taxi,' she said. 'We'll get drenched if we walk.'

'Right,' he smiled and she thought that he looked relieved. Perhaps he'd had similar thoughts to hers. 'I'll book one. Where to?'

'River's End.'

His mouth quirked at the corners. 'Sounds romantic.'

'It is rather.' She was almost tempted then to tell him that she lived on a houseboat, but something stopped her.

He went off to phone for a taxi.

While he was gone, she wondered what he would think of *Luciana*. He was a conventional man; a substantial detached residence would be more in his line. And yet was he so conventional? His idea for a teenagers' health club was far from being that. It was revolutionary, the idea of giving young people a say in their future health. Would it go down with his more conservative colleagues? Would they think the expense in time and money worth while? That was the first hurdle that he would have to overcome, and then there were the parents and the schools, who would have to be won over. . . Her thoughts broke off as he arrived back at the table. 'Taxi will be here in a few minutes,' he said.

'Thank you, and thank you for a lovely evening, and my delicious dinner.'

'Which you only half tasted. Sorry about that.'

'Don't be. I thoroughly enjoyed hearing about your project. I think it's got lots of potential. I'll give it my best shot.'

'I know you will.'

A taxi drew up in front of the building. 'I expect this is mine,' said Chloe, moving quickly across the terrace.

Ben joined her in a few short strides, and side by side they went down the steep steps leading to the pavement. She faltered as they neared the bottom, the heel of her sandal catching the step above. His hand came out immediately and was beneath her elbow, steadying her.

She found his touch electric. To her surprise and annoyance, it made her shiver. 'Thank you, but I'm perfectly all right,' she said sharply, easing her elbow from his hand. 'I just caught my heel——'

'And would have fallen flat on your face,' he interrupted drily.

'But for you,' Chloe said with a wry smile. 'Thank you, Sir Galahad, for coming to my rescue.'

He smiled. 'It was a pleasure,' he said.

He held the door open as she climbed into the taxi. 'And thanks for being such a good listener,' he said.

'I couldn't have asked for a better or more informed audience. My grateful thanks.' He stepped back from the kerb, and closed the cab door.

'Goodnight, Chloe, sleep well,' he murmured softly as the cab pulled away, and the first few spots of thundery rain fell on the hot, dusty pavement.

CHAPTER FOUR

THE thunderstorm raged for most of the night, but in spite of having very little sleep Chloe got up at her usual time of half-past six, feeling extraordinarily bright and cheerful. Her waking thought was that dinner with Ben Masters had been a success, and his enthusiasm for his teenagers' club infectious. She recalled how his stern features had lit up as he talked about the benefits such a club might bring. There had been nothing cynical or world-weary about him then; his desire to help these young people had simply revealed a deeply caring and practical doctor. And a very attractive man, when he let down his guard a little.

An unexpected wave of pleasure washed over her at the thought that she would soon be seeing him again at the centre. Would he, she wondered, be looking forward to seeing her? The thought pulled her up short. Why should he? They'd only had dinner together, a working dinner at that, two colleagues taking a meal together, nothing exceptional about it at all. It had been a pleasant evening, spent mostly talking shop, and she had been allowed to glimpse something of the warmer man concealed behind the chilly façade. She must remember that and keep things in perspective, and not expect to find a completely changed Dr Masters this morning, waiting to greet her with metaphorically open arms.

But her buoyant, almost elated mood persisted. She

sprang out of bed, pulled back the pretty rose-patterned curtains at her bedroom window, and let the warm sunshine pour in. It was going to be another glorious day, but fresher, more invigorating after the storm. Everything glistened in the early morning sunlight. The river, which had been a mass of churning water last night, was now a smooth sheet, tinted gold. Raindrops, tiny glittering prisms of coloured light, hung on the trees and hedge that lined the riverbank beyond the towpath. The air smelt like sweet white wine, and mingled with the rich scent from the honeysuckle that framed her window. A heady mixture.

The calm following the storm, she thought, smiling to herself. She lifted her arms above her head and stretched. Life felt especially good today—it was as if something spicy had been added to her usual quiet contentment.

She showered and breakfasted, and made her way through the early morning, market-day traffic, along the clean, rain-washed streets to the other side of town.

Driving into the centre car park, she saw, with an unexpected skip of a heartbeat, that Ben's Volvo was already parked. Feeling ridiculously elated, she made her way into the building, exchanging greetings with several other people arriving for work. Of Ben there was no sign, and she noted, with a little dart of disappointment, that his consulting-room door was closed. Pity; she would have liked to have wished him good morning. How silly, she thought crossly, to mind that she couldn't; their paths would cross sooner or later during the day.

As always, she was busy from the moment that she sat down at her desk, and work claimed her attention and drove all personal thoughts out of her mind. Her phone seemed to ring every few minutes, and a stream of people appeared at her door with a host of queries.

At eleven o'clock Sue Ford appeared, bearing two steaming mugs.

'Thought that as you are obviously up to your eyes in it, and hadn't put in an appearance in the staff-room, I'd play the Good Samaritan,' she said cheerfully.

'Oh, you angel, just what I need.' Chloe accepted one of the mugs and took a sip of coffee. 'Mmm, lovely.'

'Right, now give.'

'Give? I don't know what you mean.'

'Spill the beans about last night, you and our cool Dr Masters. The grape-vine's positively buzzing.'

'How on earth. . .?'

'Oh, come on, Chloe, don't be so naïve—privacy, in a town like Chidhurst! You must be joking. Some-body saw you on the terrace of the Castle Arms, taking an aperitif with our formidable Ben Masters. You didn't really think you would get away without being seen, did you?'

'Well, to be honest, I didn't really think about it. If you must know, it was purely a business meeting, a working dinner.'

Sue burst out laughing. 'Pull the other one,' she said, with raised eyebrows.

'I'm telling you,' said Chloe, 'because it's true. Honestly, he wanted to talk to me about a project that he has in mind. We couldn't fit in a meeting here because I was relieving Joy yesterday afternoon, and he simply asked me out for a working dinner. And

that, my dear nosy old Sue, is the truth, and you can
pass it on for what it's worth.'

'Well, what a let-down, and we all thought that he'd
fallen for your charms, and was in hot pursuit. The
iceman has gone into action, we thought.'

'Well, you thought wrong, he was just pursuing me
for my professional clout rather than my personal
charms.'

'Pity, but, that said, what was he like as an escort?
Was he very formal and correct?'

'Well, at first, then he unbent considerably, and we
chatted about all sorts of things. He's got a wonder-
fully dry sense of humour.'

'So did you learn anything interesting about him?'

'Only that he's house-hunting, and wants to settle
here in Chidhurst for the foreseeable future.'

'Oh, I could shake you, Lucas,' Sue said crossly.
'Didn't you find out if he's seeing anyone? After all,
he's divorced, and footloose and fancy-free, as far as
we know.'

'We didn't talk about anything that personal. As a
matter of fact, I was quite surprised when he told me
he was house-hunting—that seemed quite a breakthrough where he was concerned.'

Sue's bright blue eyes sparkled. 'Perhaps he'll ask
for your help to choose the right house—you know,
woman's touch and all that.'

'Don't be crazy. He's probably got a gorgeous
female tucked away somewhere who will suddenly
appear to do just that.'

'Yes,' agreed Sue cheerfully, 'probably the next Mrs
Masters is waiting in the wings ready to take pos-
session of him and the house. I bet beneath that icy
reserve there's a hot-blooded, passionate male just

waiting to get out for the right woman. I can't see a sexy, masculine man like him remaining womanless for long.'

'No, nor I,' Chloe replied flatly, surprised to receive a little jolt of displeasure at the idea. What on earth does it matter to me, she thought, if he's got a whole army of woman waiting to take up residence with him? 'Anyway, whatever our Dr Masters is up to, it's none of our business, Sue. I'm up to my eyes in work, I just must get on. Thanks for bringing the coffee. Much appreciated.'

'Right,' said Sue good-naturedly. 'I know when I'm dismissed from the managerial presence. Anyway, I'm busy too, I've a postnatal clinic to prepare for my *lord* and, dare I say it, *Masters*, this afternoon.'

It was in the middle of the sluggishly hot afternoon that a young lad of about thirteen was brought in on the point of collapse.

Chloe was in reception talking to Betty when the casualty arrived, supported by two scared-looking boys. In broken, excited tones they explained that they had been playing football in the nearby park when their friend had almost fainted. He had rallied sufficiently to walk to the centre with help, but was again on the point of collapse.

'Bring him through to the treatment-room,' instructed Chloe, leading the way. And to Betty, 'Call one of the doctors and tell them that I might need their help. I believe it's probably a case of heat exhaustion.'

'There's only Dr Masters in doing postnatal; the others are out on call.'

'OK, put him in the picture.'

The boys, almost carrying their friend, followed Chloe and put him on the couch as she instructed. His eyes were closed, his face pale and clammy with sweat, his breathing fast and shallow. Chloe felt for his radial pulse and found it rapid and weak. Almost certainly he was suffering from heat exhaustion. She raised the foot of the couch slightly, and the boy's eyes flickered open. He looked at her for a moment in a puzzled, unfocused fashion, and then his eyelids drooped closed again.

'What's your friend's name?' she asked the boys.

'Robin,' they said in unison. 'Robin Smith.'

'Well, Robin's conscious, thank goodness, but he's suffering from too much sun and he's dehydrated. You did the right thing bringing him in. It was very sensible of you.' The boys, who had been looking scared, looked pleased at being praised. She moved across to the basin and filled a beaker with cold water, and returned to the couch. 'Now,' she said, as she moistened Robin's lips with a gauze swab dipped in the water, 'you two can make yourselves useful again, by giving the receptionist details of Robin's address, and a phone number if you know it—that'll be a help.'

'He's my cousin; he's staying with me, and so's his mum,' said one of the boys.

'Do you think she'll be at home now?'

The boy nodded.

'Then, without alarming her too much, will you ring and tell her what's happened, and ask her to come to the surgery? You may tell the receptionist that you have my permission to use the phone. Can you do that?'

Another nod and the boys hurried from the room, leaving her with her patient.

Chloe switched the electric fan on to 'Cool', and directed it towards him. She bent over the couch. 'Robin, can you hear me?' she asked.

His eyes opened again. 'Yes,' he croaked.

Chloe smiled reassuringly. 'Here, have a sip of water.' She raised his head and held the glass to his lips. He took two big gulps, and then looked around him.

'Where. . .am I?' he asked in a puzzled, still croaky, voice.

'In the health centre—your friends brought you in from the park a few minutes ago. Do you remember that?'

'Oh. . .yeah, I remember. . . I sort of collapsed, didn't I?'

'Yes, you were exhausted by the heat. Here, have some more water.'

She was holding the beaker to his lips again when she heard footsteps in the corridor. A moment later, Ben appeared. He stood for a moment in the doorway and then crossed to the couch. Her heartbeat quickened. Ridiculous. She frowned at him. 'Thanks for coming,' she said briskly.

Ben raised his eyebrows in surprise, not understanding the frown and the briskness. She couldn't be bothered by having to deal with a case of heat exhaustion unaided. He said calmly, with a wide reassuring smile, 'Sorry I couldn't come sooner, I was in the middle of a PV examination, and your message didn't sound too urgent. I understood you could cope for a bit.'

'Yes, of course I could cope, thank you. I guessed you would come as soon as you could,' she replied stiffly, cursing her manner. What was the matter with her? Why couldn't she be natural with him? She had been hoping to see him all day, and now that he was here, smiling and pleasant, she was being almost rude to him. She was acutely conscious of his tall, broad presence as he loomed large over her and the small boy on the couch. She turned her attention to her patient and said, a little breathlessly, 'This young man, Robin Smith, appears to be suffering from heat exhaustion. He collapsed while playing football. I'm keeping him cool and giving him cold water to drink, but I think he'll need a little saline in his next drink; he's sweating quite a bit.'

'Yes, he is, isn't he?' said Ben, placing long, sensitive fingers on Robin's forehead, and then on his wrist. 'How are you feeling, old chap?'

'My legs are hurting. . .and I feel a bit sick.'

Ben said gently, taking the boy's pulse, 'Too much sun and exercise, I'm afraid, but we'll soon have you feeling better.' He turned to Chloe. 'A textbook case of mild cramps and nausea. You were right, definitely some saline indicated.'

Chloe nodded. 'I have some isotonic saline already made up,' she said, fetching a bottle from the wall cupboard on the other side of the room.

'Such efficiency,' he said, and she couldn't decide whether he was being sarcastic or complimentary.

'Basic stuff,' she said brightly.

'Quite.' He looked back down at the boy on the couch, and gave him a reassuring smile. 'Robin, we're going to give you a drink of water with a small amount of salt in it, to counteract your dehydration and help get rid of the muscle cramps in your legs.'

'All right.' Obediently he sipped the weak solution of saline that Chloe held to his lips.

Supporting the boy as he drank, Ben asked, 'Have we made contact with Robin's parents?'

'Yes, his mother has been telephoned.'

'Right, I'll have a word with her when she comes. Meanwhile I'll just have a listen to Robin's chest, and take his blood-pressure and temperature.' He ran his stethoscope over the young, sun-reddened torso, muttered, 'That's fine,' and then slipped the cuff of the sphygmomanometer round the boy's upper arm and proceeded to take his blood-pressure. 'That's not far off normal,' he said. 'Now your temperature, old chap.' He put a thermometer in Robin's mouth. 'We may find it up a little.' After half a minute, he read the thermometer. 'Thirty-seven point five, good, not much above normal.' He looked across at Chloe. 'Do you think we might do something about this first-degree sunburn, Sister?' he queried, looking up and meeting her eyes.

His gaze for a moment was intense, and she felt her cheeks redden, but she replied calmly, 'What about some lacto-calamine lotion? That should do the trick.'

He nodded. 'Good idea, simple but effective. Do try it, and then just carry on with the cooling treatment and fluid replacement.' He glanced at his watch. 'I'd best be getting back to my waiting mums, but let me know when Mrs Smith gets here, and I'll speak to her.'

At that moment, the internal phone rang. It was Betty to say that Mrs Smith had arrived.

'Right, send her along straight away,' said Ben. 'I'll see her here.'

Mrs Smith was a small pretty woman with reddish fair hair and a fair skin like her son. She was naturally anxious and concerned but, after greeting Robin, and confirming that he was improving, listened calmly as Ben told her what she must do when she got the boy home.

'Make him rest, and give him plenty of sweet, cold drinks with a pinch of salt added, while he's still sweating,' he explained. 'When he stops sweating, stop the salt, but continue with the sweet drinks. He may suddenly complain of feeling shivery and cold—this can happen. If it does, give him a *hot* sweet drink, and wrap him in a blanket until he feels comfortably warm, but is not over heated. I think you'll find that he'll be on the mend in a couple of hours or so. But if his temperature goes up suddenly, let us know at once. Not,' he finished with a smile, but firmly, 'that I think that's likely to happen, as he's already responding to treatment and is less dehydrated.' He turned to Robin. 'How are the legs feeling now?' he asked.

'Better, thanks, Doctor, and I've stopped feeling sick.'

'Good. Your mother will be able to take you home soon. Sister will tell you when you can go. Now I must get back to my clinic, Mrs Smith, so I'll say goodbye and good luck with Robin. Next time he goes off playing football in hot weather, make sure he's wearing a hat, is smothered in sunscreen cream, and has a bottle of water with him. That way you will avoid a repeat of today's episode, and also prevent the burning of that fair skin of his. By the way, you should treat Robin's chest and back with calamine lotion. Sister will let you have some.' He raised a hand in casual farewell to Mrs Smith and Robin, and nodded to Chloe. 'I'll be off now, Sister; you know where to find me if you need me,' he said drily, as he disappeared through the doorway. She heard his footsteps fading as he walked down the corridor.

The room seemed very empty after he had gone, and the oddest feeling of loneliness swept over her. For a moment she stared unseeingly at Robin's sunburnt chest.

'Sister, is there anything else I should know,' asked Mrs Smith, breaking into her reverie, 'beside what the doctor told me?'

Chloe pulled herself together. She was at work, for heaven's sake, and patients came first, not personal meanderings. She smiled at Mrs Smith. 'Dr Masters covered most points, I think, but there is one thing that you might look out for. When Robin first starts passing water, you may find that this is very dark and concentrated. Don't worry—that's because he was dehydrated, and as he drinks and absorbs more fluid to replace that which he has lost, the colour and volume of his urine output will improve.'

'Right, I'll look out for that, or tell him to. You know what boys of his age are, very secretive and sensitive, but he's very sensible. If he knows what to look out for, he will.'

Twenty minutes later Chloe judged that Robin was fit enough to go home. With help from herself and Mrs Smith he was able to walk through to Reception, where his friends were still waiting for him. At Chloe's suggestion, Mrs Smith brought her car as near to the front door as possible and, with the willing assistance of his friends, Robin made it safely to the car.

'What we need in this place,' said Betty to Chloe as she came back into reception after waving her patient off, 'is a wheelchair, or an ambulance chair, for emergencies like this. I know it doesn't happen very often that people can't walk under their own steam, but it's a problem when it does.'

Chloe stopped short by the glassed-in counter. 'Betty, what a brilliant idea. Now why didn't I think of that?'

'At a guess,' said Betty laconically, 'I would say that it is because labour-saving devices for you and your staff are not a number one priority, but I think in this case it's justified.'

'So do I,' agreed Chloe, 'thanks for the tip.'

'You're welcome.'

After tidying the clinic-room, Chloe returned to her office, determined to attack her 'housekeeping' accounts for the month and prepare them for tomorrow's staff meeting. But try as she might, she couldn't concentrate on work. She found herself shuffling invoices around aimlessly, and being unable to focus on her purchases ledger.

Her mind was full of Ben Masters and her spontaneous reaction to him. It was one thing consciously to enjoy his company as she had last evening, and even to anticipate with pleasure meeting him this morning, but it was disturbing to find her heart lurching of its own accord, as it had when he had appeared this afternoon. She disliked not being in control of her reactions. And something similar had happened earlier, she recalled, when she had been talking to Sue, and had found herself involuntarily resenting the fact that Ben probably had a woman tucked away somewhere. This was just not on. What did it matter if he had a dozen women in tow? All she wanted was to be friendly with him and break down his reserve; she wasn't looking for any other closer entanglements. No man was going to take over her life again, as Mark had once done. That sort of trusting relationship was too painful, and she had no intention of repeating it.

Relief flooded over her as she reached this decision, and she was at last able to get stuck into her work.

It was nearly seven o'clock when she decided to pack up for the day. She had done a good evening's work, and could go home with a clear conscience.

There were still a couple of patients waiting to be seen when she passed through Reception. Cathy Formby, one of Betty's young, but reliable assistants, was on duty and wished her goodnight.

'Goodnight, Cathy.' She paused at the desk. 'Who's still working?'

'The boss man himself,' she said, referring to Dr Murray, the senior partner. 'He had a big list tonight, but he's nearly finished now; he shouldn't be long.'

'Everyone else gone?'

'Yes, although Dr Masters has only just left.'

'Right, then I'll be on my way.'

She let herself out into the car park and made her way to her car. Resolutely she tried not to look towards Ben's usual parking space, but couldn't help seeing, out of the corner of her eye, that he was still there. Infuriatingly, her pulses raced at the sight of him. He was standing, very tall and lean and wide-shouldered, beside the Volvo, looking at what she guessed was a map spread out on the bonnet.

He called across as she unlocked the Peugeot, and she was forced to look up and acknowledge him. He waved a sheaf of papers at her. 'Going house-hunting—wish me luck.' He was smiling and relaxed, as he had been in the clinic-room. Perhaps last night's loosening-up process was having an effect after all.

'Good luck,' she called back quietly. 'Hope you find

what you're looking for.' She unlocked the car door
and lowered the window.

'Thanks. I have hopes—a couple of new properties
came in today.'

'Splendid. Well. . .goodnight,' she said lamely, as
she got into her car. What else could she say? She had
a feeling that he was expecting something more. That
he wanted to engage her interest. Or was that wishful
thinking on her part? 'Oh, and let me know how you
get on,' she added, as she switched on the engine.

'I might do just that. Who knows?' he said with a
deep and unexpected rumble of laughter, 'I might
need a second opinion. Goodnight.' He saluted her
with the sheaf of papers, and turned back to his map.

Had he meant that? she wondered, as she drove out
of the car park, and into the still-busy high street. If
he did, it was uncanny, so nearly like the 'woman's
touch' that Sue had thought he might need. Did it
mean that he hadn't got a woman around to please or
advise? Perhaps he was, after all, a man on his own,
without any ties. She found that the possibility
intrigued and annoyed her at one and the same time.
By the time she arrived back at River's End, she was,
against her better judgement, giving this likely scen-
ario house-room, and admitting that she liked the idea
of Ben's being fancy-free. Not that she wanted him as
anything more than a friend, she reminded herself.

She let herself into the cabin and quickly showered
and changed. She was wondering what to have to eat
when the phone rang. It was her neighbours, Paul and
Mary Watts, inviting her for drinks and supper on
their sundeck.

'Lovely,' she said. 'I'll come over now.'

She slipped her bare feet into rope-soled sandals

and made her way along the bank to their houseboat, *The Talleyrand*.

'We saw you come home,' said Mary in her motherly fashion, as Chloe went aboard, 'and thought that you looked tired.'

'What'll you drink?' asked Paul.

'Oh, a gin and tonic, please, with lots of tonic and ice.'

Paul mixed her drink and handed it to her. 'They work you too hard at the centre,' he said, 'all these long days that you do.'

'You only notice it because you're retired now, and anyway I wouldn't change it for anything.' She sat down at the table, and let herself relax. For once she was glad that she wasn't to be alone with her thoughts for the evening. 'This is nice,' she said. 'Thanks for inviting me. I was wondering what to do for my supper.'

'It's only ham, pickles and jacket potatoes,' said Mary, 'but who wants to cook in this hot weather?'

'Not I,' said Chloe, 'and this is delicious.'

They ate their supper and talked easily in the manner of old friends, and watched the ever-changing scene on the river from their vantage point. The towpath was busy, with holidaymakers from the caravan park making their way towards the Pike and Catcher, the local pub. The river itself was busy too, with a variety of tiny craft, rowing-boats and canoes being manipulated with varying degrees of skill. It was like watching a moving picture, and Chloe thought, as she so often did, how lucky she was to be living on the river, and with such delightful neighbours as Mary and Paul.

From the sundeck of *The Talleyrand*, which was

much higher than *Luciana*'s, it was possible to glimpse through the trees some of the houses that backed on to the river. They were roomy, substantial properties with large gardens, and gates in the hedges allowing access to the towpath. In one of the gardens a barbecue was in progress. In the next, just a little way up from *The Talleyrand*, two men were standing side by side, looking up at the back of the house. They were clearly visible through a gap in the trees. One was short and portly, the other tall and lean.

Chloe stared, and breathed in sharply. 'I don't believe it,' she said explosively. 'It can't be.' She was conscious of her heart thumping madly, and felt the colour come and go in her cheeks. She hoped it wasn't too obvious.

'What don't you believe?' asked Paul, as both he and Mary looked at her in some surprise.

Chloe swallowed, and managed what she hoped sounded like a casual laugh. 'That I know one of those men in that garden,' she said, pointing towards the garden in question. 'He's the new doctor at the health centre. It just surprised me, that's all, seeing him there. I knew he was house-hunting, but I didn't know that there was anything for sale in Riverside Drive.'

'It's Poynters,' said Paul. 'The house that's been let for some time. You know the owners, the Clarks, moved abroad, but didn't know whether they'd settle, so kept the house on. I heard recently that they had decided to stay in Spain, and the house is now going to be sold, but I don't think it's been advertised yet. Of course these houses go like hot cakes, and are never on the market for long. Perhaps old Dr Murray, who is friendly with the Clarks, put in a word for your new man.'

'I think that would be quite possible,' said Chloe faintly, her eyes following the two men in the garden until they disappeared from sight behind the overhanging branches of trees as they walked back towards the house.

Dusk began to fall, but it was still warm, and the Wattses and Chloe remained on the sundeck. The conversation turned naturally toward housing in general in Chidhurst, and the possibility of Poynters being sold in particular.

'Your new doctor chappy seems to have gone,' said Mary after a while. 'The lights have gone out in the house—he must have finished looking round.'

'Yes,' agreed Chloe, accepting another cup of fragrant coffee, 'he must have done.' She was beginning to get over the shock of seeing Ben Masters so close to home.

'I wonder if he will buy Poynters? It would be rather nice for you to have a friend from the centre living nearby.'

'Would it?' said Chloe, caught off guard. 'I wonder?'

Mary gave her a funny look. 'Don't you like the new doctor?' she asked, in her blunt fashion.

'Oh yes, of course, he's a very good doctor, but I don't know him very well—he's rather reserved.'

'Well, if he comes to live here it will give you a chance to get to know him better. I'm sure he will be pleased to have someone he knows as a near neighbour.'

Would he be pleased, Chloe wondered, or dismayed at finding a member of the centre staff on his doorstep? In spite of the mini-breakthrough that had occurred the night before, and his more relaxed manner today, she was still not sure what his reaction might be.

But she said diplomatically, 'Yes, I expect he will be.'

'Well, if he does move in, you must tell him that he and his family will have a warm welcome on *The Talleyrand*,' said Paul cheerfully, with his usual generosity. 'Be nice to have some new faces around.'

'Well, I'll tell him,' she promised, 'but as far as I know he hasn't any family. He's divorced.'

'He must be planning to marry again,' said Mary. 'Otherwise, why would he be interested in a family house like Poynters? Perhaps that's why he seems so cagey.'

'Yes, perhaps,' Chloe said quietly.

She didn't want to talk about it any more, and felt quite suddenly that she wanted to be alone with her churning thoughts. She declined yet another cup of the aromatic coffee, said her goodnights and thank-yous, and returned along the footpath, in the warm scented darkness, to *Luciana* and bed.

Bed, but not to sleep. Sleep eluded her. The idea that Ben Maters might be moving into Riverside Drive was too disturbing. She didn't know whether she wanted him to or not. One part of her was excited at the prospect of seeing more of him, another part recoiled from the possibility. He was an attractive man, and she felt herself being drawn to him against her will, which was a ridiculous situation to be in, at her age and with her experience. All her instincts told her to steer clear of him. As Sue, and this evening Mary, had suggested, he probably wasn't free anyway, and was planning to remarry. Otherwise, why would he be considering buying a house big enough to house a family? Why indeed?

She sat up and punched and turned her hot pillow. It's none of your business, she told herself. Forget the man, just remember that he's a colleague and a damned good doctor, and get your feelings under control.

On this thought, she finally fell asleep.

CHAPTER FIVE

FOR Chloe, the weeks that followed her supper with the Wattses, and her sighting of Ben in the garden, flew by.

She had never been so busy, keeping up with her paperwork and covering her colleagues' holidays. She had little time to think during duty hours about her evening out with Ben Masters, or the possibility that he might be planning to buy a house in Riverside Drive. Occasionally she wondered if he might follow up their working dinner with a further invitation, but when he didn't, she was almost relieved. She had yet to come to terms with the fact that he affected her more than she liked, whenever she saw him. Why did her heart flutter uncontrollably and her pulses race at the sight of him? Was it some primitive chemistry at work? She had no sensible answer as to why she should respond to him in such a fashion, when all she wanted from the man was simple friendship, nothing more. In time, she convinced herself, her feelings would pass, and she would stop behaving so irrationally.

So she reassured herself during those last hot days of June, as she tackled one job after another with her usual enthusiasm and determination.

A gloriously tanned and well-rested Alison Knight returned to work and resumed her care of the ante and postnatal clinics.

Ben was only too pleased to hand these clinics back

to her, as his paediatric list was beginning to build up with children being referred by his colleagues. His general list, too, increased, as automatically new patients were passed on to him. He was fast becoming one of the busiest doctors in the practice, but he seemed to thrive on it and, although still aloof at times, was generally more approachable.

'He's a gem to work with,' said Sue. 'He's marvellous with the mums and babes, and the mums-to-be in the clinic; they're going to miss him. Though he's still keeping an eye on the infants in postnatal. And you were right about him having a dry sense of humour, Chloe. It often popped up when he was working.'

It was at the end of June that he appeared at Chloe's office door, and her heart, to her annoyance, flipped of its own accord when she saw him. 'Have you got a minute?' he asked.

'Of course,' she replied evenly, pleased with her outward calm. 'Do come in and sit down.'

'Thanks.' He seated himself opposite her. 'I won't keep you long. I wanted to let you know that, as from Tuesday week, I will have a new address, which I presume you will need for your records.'

'You've found a house!' She tried to keep her voice steady, devoid of excitement, telling herself that it didn't matter where he lived, yet illogically, she found herself hoping. . .

'Yes, I'm pleased to say that I have. It's a house in Riverside Drive, called Poynters. I shall be taking over the phone that's already there—here's the number, although, of course, I can still be contacted on my mobile phone.'

She made a note of the information. 'How nice,' she said brightly. 'We will be near neighbours. I live on a houseboat at River's End, almost at the bottom of your garden. The river runs parallel to the Drive.'

'Yes, it will be pleasant to be near the river,' he said, with a smile that warmed his grey eyes. 'And what a bonus having you as a neighbour,' he added softly, staring intently at her across the desk.

'Thank you,' she murmured. His eyes seemed to compel her to look at him, and for breathless moments she felt that she was drowning, drowning in their grey-blue bottomless depths as he held her in an intense, hypnotic gaze. The rest of his features blurred, only his eyes remaining in focus. A deep silence hung between them like a tangible thing. The air was electric.

Then he spoke again, softly, and it was as if his voice came from a long way off. 'How nice to know that I will have a friend on the spot when I move in, someone who can introduce me to the important amenities, like my local for instance,' he said, as his eyes continued to bore into hers and hold her captive.

At last Chloe let out a long sigh and blinked, and the magnetic spell broke suddenly and she found her voice. 'It'll be a pleasure to show you around,' she said huskily. She cleared her throat, and in a more normal voice said, 'In fact, why not come along to the Pike and Catcher tonight? We've got a darts match on. The pub's only about half a mile from Poynters; you'll find it easily enough. I'll introduce you to a few people before you actually move in.'

'Thank you, I should like that. If I can get away, I will.' He looked at his watch, scraped back his chair and stood up. 'I must let you get on,' he said, suddenly brisk. 'Until this evening, then,' and with an almost curt nod of his head he left the room, closing the door quietly behind him.

Chloe sat staring at the closed door, her mind a seething jumble of thoughts. Her heart was pumping away furiously, her respirations were fast and shallow. She took a few deep, deliberate breaths as she tried to get control of herself. What had all that been about? What on earth had happened between them, with that long, searching, silent exchange? It was as if, for a moment, they had looked deep into each other's souls where words were not necessary. But how could it happen with someone whom she scarcely knew, someone whom she thought of as almost a stranger? And yet, briefly, as she looked into his eyes, she felt that she had known Ben Masters forever.

It was ridiculous and a little frightening. They had seemed for a moment so much at one with each other. In spite of the heat of the afternoon, she shivered. Somehow she must put it out of her mind, and get on with her work, be practical. It was ludicrous to be so disturbed just by a look. You're probably exaggerating what happened anyway, she told herself, and it's only significant in your own mind. Stop letting your imagination run away with you. You just looked at the man, and he looked at you. So what!

With a great effort of will, she was, by the end of the day, almost able to convince herself that this was what had happened, and nothing of significance had passed between them. But deep inside herself she knew this wasn't true—something *had* happened, and she wondered, with a little *frisson* of excitement, how Ben would react to her when they met, *if* they met, that evening. And how would she respond to him?

Her heart hammered uncontrollably at the thought, but her mind was a blank.

In the event, when Ben arrived at the Pike and Catcher, he seemed to be, as usual, quite unruffled. He was casually dressed in an open-necked sports shirt and dark blazer over pale cotton trousers.

She had schooled herself to be calm and relaxed, but she was very conscious of his lean, dark, charismatic presence beside her as she introduced him to her friends. The women, as always, were attracted to him as to a magnet; even her sane, sensible friend Mary seemed to glow when he spoke to her in his deep, melodious voice. But, more surprisingly, the men too seemed to take to him, and Chloe realised that for the first time since she had known him he appeared to have dropped his barrier of reserve. Was it perhaps because he was away from the surgery, she wondered, or was there some other reason?

The evening was a great success. Everyone made him welcome, and Paul and Mary Watts, as always, were particularly friendly.

Later, as they stood outside the pub under a clear sky dusted with stars, wishing each other goodnight, Paul said, 'What a pity that we'll be away on holiday when you move in, Ben. Mary and I, being put out to grass, and having all the time in the world, could have given you a hand.'

'Yes, or we could at least have plied you with food and drink,' added Mary. 'It's hell moving house, especially on your own. Let's just hope that the weather keeps fine for you.'

'I certainly hope so,' Ben agreed. 'Thanks for the thought—your help would have been appreciated—

and thanks for making me so welcome tonight. Do have a good holiday. See you when you get back, by which time I shall be safely installed. Goodnight.'

'Goodnight,' they said in unison, and to Chloe, 'We'll see you presently—catch us up along the towpath.' They seemed to take it for granted that she would want to say a separate goodnight to Ben. They turned and walked away, leaving Ben and Chloe alone in the deserted car park.

It was very quiet after the Wattses had gone. A still, clear night. Ben looked down at her and, in the light still streaming out from the pub windows, she saw that he was smiling. She smiled back into his eyes. He reached out and took both her hands in his and squeezed them gently. 'Chloe, what can I say but thank you for a super evening, and for introducing me to so many people? What a nice crowd they are.' Chloe was conscious of the pressure on her hands increasing as he said, 'We must do this again soon, have an evening out together.'

'I should like that very much,' she replied rather breathlessly.

'Good.' His voice was low and soft, intimate. 'I owe you a proper dinner. The last time I monopolised you over the teenagers' health club.'

'It doesn't matter,' she said, though her heart bounded at his tone. 'The clinic is important. Once you've got settled in your new house, then perhaps we can have an evening out,' she murmured.

'Yes, we'll fix something.' Fleetingly, his steel-grey eyes held a gentle, tende. expression. He inclined his head slightly, and for one euphoric moment she thought that he was going to kiss her. Then, as swiftly as it had come, the tender expression in his eyes faded

and was replaced by a sardonic gleam. He said in a
matter-of-fact voice, 'Meanwhile, I must say goodnight. Pity about that, but I'm on call from midnight.'
He let go her hands and she let them fall to her sides.

Chilled by his sudden change of manner, Chloe said
stiffly, 'You'd better go, then. Goodnight.'

'Goodnight, Chloe, and once again, thank you.'

He ignored her stiffness and gave her a friendly
smile, and then, lifting his hand in salute, turned away
and walked towards his car.

As the days passed, Chloe found herself, against her
will, longing for Ben to give some sign, after that
evening at the pub, that he wanted to get to know her
better. But he made no such sign; he remained
friendly but aloof. She hardly liked to admit it, could
barely understand it, but his apparent indifference
actually hurt.

But was he indifferent? There were occasions, when
they met in the staff-room or in reception with other
people about, when she was conscious of him watching
her; and his eyes had seemed to meet hers with a
challenging intensity, as if he wanted to say something
and couldn't, or wouldn't.

Or was it all in her imagination? In her present state
of uncertainty she had no way of knowing. She continued to apply herself to work when she was on duty,
but off duty she felt lost, disorientated and, for the
first time in years, lonely, bereft, just as she had when
she had learned of Mark's infidelity. She felt helpless,
and as if she was in a sort of no man's land.

Flaming June gave way to a wet July, and it poured
with rain on the Tuesday that Ben was due to move

into Poynters. Chloe, finding herself with adequate staff for a brief period, due to somebody's altered holiday plans, was taking a few long-overdue days off. She might have known it would be rotten weather, both for her holiday and Ben's move.

She pulled back her curtains and stared out at the river, churning yellowly under the onslaught of wind and rain.

Should she have offered to help him with the move, when she knew she was going to be off duty? It would have been the friendly and neighbourly thing to do. Friendly, neighbourly, hmm? She was loath to admit it, but deep in her heart, she knew that one part of her simply wanted an excuse to be near him, and it had nothing to do with being neighbourly; only some instinct, some fear of being rebuffed, had prevented her making the offer. Not that there was any reason to suppose that he would have rebuffed her; common sense told her that he would simply have accepted help as a friendly gesture.

Only she was aware that there would have been more to it than that. Her heart beat unsteadily at the thought, and irritably she told herself not to be an idiot. She wasn't a schoolgirl, to be attracted to every presentable man, and think herself in love with him. In love! In love with Ben Masters! The idea was too ridiculous for words.

For a start, how could you be in love with a man whom you scarcely knew and at times didn't like? 'Well, you can't be, and you're not,' she muttered firmly, with a touch of irony. 'Stick to being just a good neighbour, a friendly colleague; it'll save you a lot of heartache.'

It wasn't too late to offer help. She knew that he

was moving in some time during the morning when his furniture arrived from London.

By mid-morning she had admitted to herself that she was glad of the excuse, any excuse, to see Ben. It was no use pretending otherwise but, just as long as he didn't know how she felt, her feelings were unimportant.

She made fresh, fragrant coffee and filled a flask, and packed a basket with ham and tomato sandwiches, and half the fruit cake she had baked the day before. She put on an old fawn raincoat and wellies, pinned up her hair beneath a waterproof yachting cap, and set off through the rain.

Heart in mouth, she let herself into Poynters via the garden gate. Through the patio terrace doors she could see several men moving about in one of the ground-floor rooms, running from the back to the front of the house, which she guessed was the sitting-room. Another door with a wide picture window beside it opened on to the terrace. Steps led from the terrace down to the garden. She stood on top of the steps and looked through the window into a large airy room that was obviously the kitchen. It was empty except for several packing-cases standing on the floor.

She rang the bell beside the door, and waited with fluttering heartbeats. A moment later, Ben appeared in the kitchen.

He recognised her through the glass door, and raised his eyebrows in a surprised fashion. At the sight of him, her courage nearly failed her. She wanted to turn and run.

He opened the door wide, and gave her one of his rare smiles.

'Why, Chloe, how nice to see you. My first visitor.

Do come in.' He stood aside to let her pass. 'I'm in a hell of a mess, as you can imagine, but you're most welcome.' His voice sounded very deep and warm and sincere, and she knew that she really was welcome.

Gingerly she stepped on to the rubber mat just inside the doorway. 'I'll take off my boots, if I may,' she said, a shade breathlessly. 'They're awfully muddy. Mustn't spoil your nice clean floor.'

'Oh, don't worry about that, it won't stay clean long today, but do take them off, you'll be more comfortable. Can you manage?'

Chloe nodded, and eased off her green wellies, standing them neatly on the mat. She handed him the plastic-covered basket. 'I've brought some real coffee,' she said with a little laugh that she hoped sounded light-hearted and casual, 'and sandwiches. I thought you might be in need of sustenance.'

'Real coffee—great, how clever of you. I haven't unearthed the kettle yet, though I did bring teabags and instant coffee from the hotel. Apparently it's obligatory to supply the removal men with endless cups of something while they're working.'

'Would you like me to unpack the kitchen stuff for you and find the kettle? Presumably it's in one of these boxes.'

'Yes, it is. Are you sure you don't mind, about unpacking?'

'Not at all. I've come to help, after all; it's what neighbours are for.'

Suddenly they were smiling into each other's eyes.

'Such nice neighbours,' he rumbled, his voice very deep. 'I'm a lucky bloke.' There was a moment's pregnant silence as they stared at each other and a stream of awareness, of belonging, passed between

them as it had once before, that day in her office,
when she had felt that she was drowning in the grey
depths of his eyes. He said softly, 'You must get out
of that wet mac, Chloe. Here, let me help you off with
it.'

'Thanks.' She half turned her back to him, and with
fingers that shook slightly undid the buttons. He eased
the mac from her shoulders, touching her with his
knuckles as he did so.

A tremor ran through her. He was going to kiss her.

'Oh, Chloe,' he said thickly, 'you look ridiculous
and quite lovely in that funny old cap—very nautical.'
She felt his warm breath on the bare skin between the
band of her cap and the scooped-out neckline of her
loose T-shirt, then his lips were pressing very gently
on the nape of her neck as he nuzzled her soft, yielding
flesh.

She stood stock-still, eyes closed, savouring the
feeling of his lips on her bare flesh, hardly daring to
breathe, not wanting the kissing to stop. She heard
him drop her raincoat on a chair, then his hands were
on her shoulders, turning her round to face him and
draw her towards him. Mutely she lifted her face to
his, longing to feel his mouth on hers. . .

A voice from the doorway asked, 'Where shall we
put this bookcase, Doc—downstairs or up?'

Momentarily Ben's hands tightened on her
shoulders. He lifted his eyebrows and gave her a
whimsical, lopsided grin. 'Downstairs, please, in the
study.'

The removal man disappeared.

Ben continued to look down at her with dark,
glowing eyes. He said drily, 'Sorry about that. Now
doesn't seem either the time or the place for kissing of

the maturer kind.' His grin broadened. With gentle fingers he tucked back under her cap a strand of hair that had escaped. 'I suggest we wait till later when we will have the house to ourselves—how does that sound?'

'Wonderful,' she whispered, smiling back at him. 'Infinitely better.' Obviously this was not the time or the place to pursue whatever lay between them. But at least she knew now that it was not all in her imagination, this magnetism that flowed between them. There was something special pulling them together, and he too was aware of it. A great tide of joy washed over her. In moments her world had changed. 'I'll make drinks for everyone,' she said, laughing. 'Just give me a few minutes to find the kettle and put it on to boil. And while I'm doing that, hadn't you better go through and direct the men, make sure that everything is where it should be?'

'Yes, Sister, ma'am,' he said with a wicked smile, giving her a sketchy salute. 'To hear is to obey.'

Chloe giggled. 'Idiot,' she said.

He walked to the door and turned. 'Don't go anywhere, love,' he said softly, a wealth of meaning in his voice. 'We have unfinished business to attend to.'

The removal men left at last, and the house was suddenly very quiet.

Ben, having seen the men off, appeared in the kitchen doorway as Chloe, perched on a stool, was stacking the last of the china in one of the cupboards.

'Clever you, you've finished unpacking this lot!' he exclaimed, looking at the empty packing-cases. 'You

must have worked like a Trojan between all that tea
and coffee-making. Thank you so much.'

Again a wave of happiness suffused her. She turned
a shining face towards him. 'I've enjoyed it, putting
things away in cupboards. I just hope you'll be able to
find everything when I've gone. It's not everyone who
would let a stranger loose in their kitchen.'

Ben strode across the tiled floor and stood looking
up at her. 'I don't consider you a stranger,' he said
quietly, his eyes meeting eyes. 'And you can give me
a conducted tour later, so that I will know where to
find everything. Meanwhile, woman,' he said, with a
laugh to take the chauvinistic sting out of his words,
'come down off your perch and give me something to
eat. I'm starving, and I could drink your flask of *real*
coffee dry.'

He was wearing a short-sleeved sports shirt, and as
he held up his bare, brown arms with their tangle of
dark, curling hairs Chloe, without thinking, slid into
them. He lowered her to the ground, and she stood
facing him, wide-eyed and expectant. 'Oh, Chloe,' he
said thickly, staring down at her.

'Ben,' she whispered. She leant against his broad,
cotton-covered chest, aware of his heart thudding
rhythmically against her soft breasts, and feeling, as
her knees quaked, that she might collapse at any
minute if his arms had not been firm about her.

He lowered his head, and she closed her eyes,
waiting for his kiss.

She could feel his warm breath fanning her face as
he came closer, hear his ragged breathing in the quiet.
His lips were almost touching hers when the telephone
shrilled into life.

They clung together for a moment in silence. The phone shrilled again.

'Damn,' he said. 'Who the hell can that be? I'm not on call.' Keeping one arm round her, he stretched out and picked up the phone. 'Yes,' he said tersely. 'Dr Masters here.' Chloe could half hear a muffled voice at the other end of the phone. Ben's arm tightened round her waist. 'Yes, of course, will do, at once. Never mind the house, it doesn't matter. And don't worry about contacting Chloe—she's here, I'll let her know.'

He switched off, laid the phone down, and let the arm that was round Chloe's waist drop. His gentler, smiling face had vanished, leaving him with his usual stern expression. He looked deadly serious. 'That was a call from the surgery,' he said flatly. 'An SOS for all off-duty medical and nursing staff to go to an accident on the bypass by the bridge. Apparently there's been a terrific pile-up involving coaches and buses as well as other vehicles. They crashed in the storm. Local services are going to be stretched until other help can be brought in. I said we'd both go.'

'Of course.' She managed a small smile. 'Let's go.' She collected her waterproof from the back of the chair and shrugged herself into it, and padded over to the door to put on her wellies.

'I'll just get my case,' Ben said, 'it's in the study.'

He returned moments later with his medical bag, and wearing a long, black belted raincoat and waterproof cap.

'Ready?' he said briskly, as if those recent tender moments had never happened.

'Quite,' Chloe replied.

* * *

They travelled in silence to the scene of the crash, each wrapped in their own thoughts, each putting behind them what had just happened between them, and preparing themselves for what was to come.

CHAPTER SIX

THEY joined the double queue of cars as they reached the dual carriageway on the outskirts of the town, and crawled along for a few minutes at a snail's pace.

'This is bloody hopeless,' said Ben through gritted teeth. 'The police must have set up a road block and be diverting people back round the town.'

'Yes, but they'll let us through when we get to the barrier,' said Chloe quietly.

'True, but at this rate when the hell will that be?' He glanced at her with sombre eyes. 'There's a load of casualties there who need us now.' He shrugged and added in a resigned voice, 'But unfortunately there's damn all we can do about it.' He wound down the window and leaned out and tried to see ahead to where the diversion might be, but all that was visible was a line of red tail-lights. Drawing his head back into the car, he glanced at his wing mirror and saw the flashing blue light of a police motorcyclist, followed by an ambulance driving on to the grassed-over central reservation. 'Right,' he said, 'we'll go in with them.'

Their line of traffic had ground almost to a stop. The policeman and ambulance were catching up with them. Ben leant out of the window again and waved them down. When the motorcycle was almost abreast of the Volvo, Ben shouted, 'We're a doctor and nurse; can you help us get through?'

'Sure, move in behind me,' called the police officer,

and he put on a spurt so that Ben could pull out of line and in between his bike and the ambulance.

As they followed their police escort along the bumpy central reservation, they became aware of a red-orange glow ahead of them, and the smell of burning rubber and hot metal filled their nostrils.

'Vehicles on fire,' Ben said tersely.

'Oh, I hadn't thought about that,' murmured Chloe. 'How awful.'

'It's going to be pretty grim altogether,' he said in a low voice. 'Have you ever been involved in a big accident before, Chloe?'

She shook her head. 'No, though I've worked in Casualty, which could be pretty horrific at times.'

'Yes, indeed,' he said, with a quick, reassuring smile, 'but be prepared for some pretty unpleasant sights, and remember that we'll only be doing first-aid with what little we've got to hand.'

Minutes later they found themselves at the heart of the accident site. A policeman had indicated where to leave their car, but beyond this initial piece of organisation all seemed to be in utter chaos. They stood for a brief moment, taking in the appalling scene.

Vehicles lay strewn singly or in clusters along the road and along the embankment. Some were on fire, in spite of the pouring rain. A pall of black smoke hung over the scene, which, mingling with the low, dark clouds, turned the July afternoon almost into night. And the noise was horrendous as fire engines and more ambulances and other service vehicles arrived on the scene. Shouted orders mingled with the cries of the injured. Blue lights flashed, and the sirens of approaching vehicles added to the general noise and confusion. There seemed to be people every-where, in uniform and out of it, some going purpose-fully about their business, some wandering aimlessly. It was a macabre scene, lit intermittently by the flashing lights and the glow from the fires.

They stood, feeling helpless, by the control vehicle to which they had been directed until suddenly, out of the gloom, a man in a hard hat and yellow fluorescent jacket approached them. He looked like someone in authority.

'I'm the chief accident officer,' he said brusquely. 'Who are you?'

'Local GP Ben Masters and Sister Lucas, health centre manager,' replied Ben.

'Thank God for that, we need more doctors and nurses. Look, start over there.' He pointed to two cars and a motorbike. 'We haven't got around to assessing that area yet. I'll send an ambulance and paramedics as soon as possible. Just do what you can.'

Ben took Chloe's hand and squeezed it hard. 'Come on,' he said firmly. 'Let's make ourselves useful—the motorcyclist first.'

The two cars were half on the roadway, half on the embankment, and the motorbike lay between them, but the rider, who looked little more than a boy, had been thrown some distance away and was lying on his back on the roadway. His helmet was badly dented and his head was twisted to one side. Blood, dirt and rain ran down his grazed face and from his nose. One leg was doubled up beneath his body at a grotesque angle.

They crouched down on either side of him and Ben pushed back the leather jacket cuff to take his radial pulse.

He frowned. 'Try your side,' he said abruptly after a few moments. 'I can't get anything here.'

Chloe placed her fingers on the young man's wrist. Nothing! She moved her fingers slightly and tried again. She couldn't believe it. There was no pulse. She stared at Ben in anguish over the still body. 'Oh, no,' she whispered, 'he can't be.'

Ben was getting his stethoscope out of his case. 'Undo his jacket,' he ordered.

Chloe tore open the leather jacket and pulled up the T-shirt beneath, exposing the lad's narrow chest. Ben, listening intently, moved his stethoscope back and forth in the region of the heart. After a while he shook his head. 'Absolutely nothing,' he said. 'I believe death was almost instantaneous: broken neck, fractured skull, probably other internal injuries. He hadn't a hope.'

'Mouth-to-mouth?'

'Too late.'

'He's so young, little more than a boy,' Chloe murmured as she fastened his jacket against the steadily falling rain. 'His poor parents, they'll be devastated.'

Ben reached out and took her hand and pulled her to her feet. 'Yes,' he said, his voice harsh. 'But there's nothing we can do about that. Come on, let's go and do what we can for the living.'

With a huge effort, Chloe pulled herself together. Ben was quite right, they had other work to do.

He led the way to the nearest car, a small four-door hatchback.

In the driver's seat sat a young woman, staring straight ahead with tears silently streaming down her face. She made no move as Ben rapped on the window, or when, with some difficulty because it was dented, he wrenched open the driver's door.

Neither did she move when Chloe opened the other door and spoke to her. 'Hello, love, we're here to help. Can you hear me?' There was no response. Chloe sat down in the passenger seat and lifted the woman's hand and took her pulse. 'Slow and thready,' she said to Ben.

Ben shone his torch into the woman's eyes, which remained wide and staring, and then ran quick, sure hands over her head, neck, arms and trunk. 'No external damage up here,' he said, 'but she's obviously in shock. Internal injuries perhaps. She's possibly been unconscious and has just come round.' He touched the pale, wet face gently, and repeated what Chloe had said. 'Hello, love, it's all right, we're here to help. I'm a doctor and this lady's a nurse.' He spoke slowly and distinctly. 'Can you tell me your name, and whether you are in pain?'

At first the woman didn't move, then slowly she turned her head and, frowning and wincing, focused on Ben. 'Where am I?' she asked in a faint voice.

'You've had an accident on the bypass near Chidhurst. Can you tell me your name and whether you have a pain anywhere?'

Her frown deepened for a moment, and then she mumbled, 'Di—Diana Bird. It's my legs that hurt; I can't move them.' She closed her eyes, screwed up her face, and suddenly fainted. Chloe released her tight seatbelt and bent her head forward as much as she dared.

Ben shone his torch into the dark area under the steering-wheel and saw that both her feet were trapped by the pedals in the caved-in front of the car. He tried to ease the seat back, but found that it had jammed forward off the runners. One leg was obviously broken below the knee: a piece of bone was sticking through the skin and the thin stockings or tights that she was wearing. The other leg was twisted and bleeding.

'An open fracture on one leg,' Ben said in a low voice to Chloe. 'Looks like the shaft of the tibia. I can't move her. It'll need firemen with cutters to do that. The best I can do is fix a clean dressing over the break, and give her a shot of morphine for the pain. Here, take my case and get them ready for me, please, while I have a listen to her chest.'

'Right.' She opened his surgical case and handed him his stethoscope.

'And then find something to put over her—we'll get her as warm as possible to counteract the shock.'

At that moment Diana came out of her faint. She frowned and a curious expression passed over her face. And then without warning she cried out, 'My baby!' She clutched at Chloe's and Ben's arms. 'Is my baby all right?'

Ben and Chloe stared at each other. A baby! Was the woman delirious?

Diana half turned in her seat, ignoring the pain that she must have felt when she moved. Her eyes were no longer vacant but fierce and intent. 'In the back, *please*,' she breathed, tightening the clutch on Chloe's arm. 'See if Fiona's all right.'

Immediately Chloe knelt on the seat and peered into the back of the car. Bags of shopping were strewn over half of the back seat, their contents partially spilling on to the floor; a tartan rug drooped untidily from the rear window-shelf covering the remaining space. Tentatively Chloe lifted a corner of the rug, and there, securely strapped into a carry-cot, lay the still form of a baby.

Her incredulous eyes met Ben's, and she nodded. 'There is a baby,' she whispered.

Diana said shrilly, 'Is Fiona all right?'

Chloe's heart thudded painfully. Was the infant dead or alive? She didn't look as though she was hurt, but one couldn't tell; she was just lying there passively like a doll, looking slightly flushed, eyes closed, long lashes on rosy cheeks.

Ben leaned over and laid his first two fingers against the fragile-looking temples. 'Amazing! Temporal pulse even, good and strong, skin normally warm,' he murmured. His eyes meeting Chloe's held a tender, relieved expression. He said gently to Diana, 'Your baby's fine, fast asleep. She hasn't a clue as to what has happened. That's babies all over—no sense of occasion.'

He smiled reassuringly at her, and she miraculously managed a small smile in return through her pain. 'I want to hold her,' she said.

'Of course, you can hold her for a moment, and then I'm going to give you an injection for the pain. It'll make you sleepy, but someone will stay with you till the ambulance arrives. Don't worry, your baby will go with you when you go.' His deep voice was confident and comforting.

Chloe unstrapped Fiona from the carry-cot and placed her in her mother's arms. Diana was seemingly oblivious to her own pain as she confirmed that her baby was safe. She held her close and kissed her soft forehead and crooned over her. Fiona stirred and made little mewing and sucking sounds, but didn't wake.

After a few moments, Ben said gently, 'Best give her back to Nurse now. I must give you your injection.'

Mutely, Diana handed the baby over to Chloe. 'Look after her for me,' she murmured, her eyes wide and appealing.

'I will.'

'As her own,' said Ben softly, as his eyes swept over Chloe and the precious bundle in her arms, and then came to rest on her face. 'As her own,' he repeated. For the briefest instant, as her eyes met Ben's, she felt that she was alone with him and the baby in spite of the carnage all around them.

The moment passed. Chloe sat cradling Fiona as Ben, working with speed and efficiency, gave Diana an injection of morphine, secured a sterile dressing over the fractured tibia, and covered her with the tartan rug.

'Stay put,' he said when he had finished. 'I'm off to get help.'

Chloe found it strange sitting cocooned in the small car watching all the activity going on around her, listening to the quiet breathing of Fiona and the deep, heavy breathing of the sedated Diana.

But she didn't have to wait long, for Ben soon returned with two firemen carrying heavy-duty cutters. She had to leave the car while the firemen worked from both sides to cut the pedals away from Diana's trapped feet, and man-handle the seat back on to the tracks so that it could be moved backwards. Diana moaned occasionally while they were working, but mercifully remained sedated.

When the firemen left, Chloe gently put the baby back in her carry-cot on the back seat. Then together she and Ben straightened Diana's injured legs as much as they were able, and bound them together to act as splints on each other. They had just finished when an ambulance stopped nearby, and the two paramedics on board approached, ready to take mother and baby to the hospital.

Together they helped install Diana and Fiona in the ambulance, and stood watching as it drove away.

Chloe said in a slightly wobbly voice, 'I hope they'll be all right.'

'I'm sure they will, love,' said Ben, reaching out and squeezing her hand. 'Now come on, let's see what we've got over here.' He strode across to a green Ford estate, that had slewed round and was facing down the embankment. Chloe followed.

They found the driver unconscious. Clearly, he had shot forward on to the steering-wheel, sustaining severe chest injuries.

'The fool,' said Ben angrily, as he examined his stove-in chest, and the mess of blood and broken bones protruding from his chest. 'He obviously wasn't wearing a seatbelt.'

'And it looks as if he had been drinking,' said Chloe, holding up a half-empty bottle of whisky. 'Oh, Ben, can we do anything for him?'

'Not much. Give him pethedine or morphine to kill the pain. He must be bleeding internally, and we can't do anything about that. We'll put a pad over his chest and secure with his left arm to support, with an elevation sling and a bandage. Let's hope he can be removed to hospital soon and get those bones fixed and have a transfusion. We won't move him more than we have to, but we'll turn him slightly on his side with the seat tilted back in a semi-recovery position.'

At that moment the senior medical officer approached and crouched down beside them. He looked down at the driver, and shook his head.

'Christ, what a mess,' he said to them both, and then to Chloe, 'I can see that you've got your hands full for the moment, Sister, but when you've finished here, will you please escort a group of people with minor injuries to your local cottage hospital? There's no casualty department there, of course, but they're opening their doors to us in this emergency. The police are arranging for a bus to take the casualties, and if you could organise treatment for them when you arrive at the hospital I'd be grateful.'

'Of course I'll go wherever I'm needed,' she said at once, suppressing a twinge of disappointment that she wouldn't be working beside Ben any more that day.

'Thanks. If you make your way to the tail-end of this mess when you're ready, you'll find most of the walking wounded grouped together. The police will help you get them on board the transport they've arranged.' He turned to Ben. 'But if you could stay on here, Dr Masters,' he said flatly, 'I'd be glad of your continuing help. In spite of having more medics on the scene, there's still plenty to do.'

'I'm free for as long as you need me,' said Ben as, with Chloe's help, he fixed a pad and a sling on their patient. 'Where do you want me next?'

'Up there on the embankment by the coach that's lying on its side. The police think it's in danger of slipping and there are still people inside, though we're getting them out as fast as we can. It was full. We suspect some crush injuries and probably a fair number of fractures.'

Ben said, 'OK, I'll be up there as soon as I've finished here.'

'Thanks.' The medical officer strode off.

Ben gave the injured driver a shot of morphine. 'That's the best we can do for him for now,' he said to Chloe, his face grim.

An ambulance drew up beside them and two paramedics jumped out. 'Right, Doc, we'll take over here,' said one of them.

'Thank God for that,' said Ben. 'He needs fluids and blood fast. He's almost certainly haemorrhaging internally.'

'We'll set up a line immediately. Will you give us a hand to get him on to the stretcher?'

Both Chloe and Ben helped place the injured man on the stretcher and watched as the paramedics moved him to the nearby ambulance.

Isolated for a few brief moments from the turmoil around them, they looked at each other through the veil of rain.

Ben stretched out a hand and tucked a strand of hair beneath the band of Chloe's yachting cap. 'I'm sorry they're splitting us up,' he said gruffly, 'we make a good team.'

Chloe blinked the rain out of her eyes. 'Yes, that's what I thought, but orders are orders. I'd better go and look after my walking wounded. At least I will soon be in the dry, whereas poor old you will still be getting drenched.'

'Can't be helped,' he said briskly. 'Now I'd best be off and make myself useful.' He raised a hand and started to move up the slope toward the coach. 'Take care,' he added quietly, speaking over his shoulder as he moved away.

'And you, you take care too,' she said to his retreating back, wondering if he had heard her. She hoped he had; there was something very tender about the phrase 'take care', and the way he had said it. Two small words that could mean so much.

She turned the words over in her mind as she picked her way through the debris towards the tail-end of the stream of accident vehicles and the patients she was to escort. She wondered why Ben had used them, and she had endorsed them. After all, they were neither of them in imminent danger. 'Take care.' They must have been inspired by the general atmosphere of death and disaster that lay all around them. It had touched even hardened professionals like themselves: so many broken bodies, so many dead, and all because somebody hadn't 'taken care'.

An hour or so later, Chloe was busy organising the care of her walking wounded. The reception hall and sitting-room of the cottage hospital were crammed to capacity with patients and willing helpers. An elderly retired doctor who occasionally acted as locum for the hospital MO had arrived ready to help out, and Chloe asked him to be responsible for giving everyone a quick check, deciding upon treatment, and where necessary giving anti-tetanus injections. He readily agreed. 'Nice to be useful,' he said.

Two downstairs bathrooms were arranged as make-shift clinic-rooms, where Chloe and the matron dressed superficial wounds, gave antibiotics, and put in the occasional stitch, as prescribed by Dr Meadows.

Two auxiliary nurses assisted, dispensing hot, sweet drinks, and generally reassuring the shocked patients.

The system worked smoothly. Dr Meadows diagnosed and sent patients through to Matron or Chloe for treatment, and as they worked they took particulars of each patient for the record.

Chloe finished stitching a long, clean cut on a young man's arm. There was no deep muscle damage. He was a local chap and on the health centre list. 'That'll be fine, Tom,' she said. 'Call in at the surgery in about a week's time and we'll probably be able to take the stitches out. Now you're sure you feel up to making your own way home?'

'I'm OK, Sister, thanks. . . God, I'm lucky compared to some people. I was on the local bus from the station which was only involved with the end of the pile-up.'

'Yes, you're quite right, it could have been much worse. But you have had a shock, Tom, so keep warm and have plenty to drink. Now will you please send in the next patient as you go out?'

'Will do,' said Tom as he left.

A few minutes later there was a tap at the door, and a girl dressed in a school uniform entered. She was about thirteen or fourteen, and was tall and slender with short dark hair and heavily fringed grey eyes. She was limping and holding a tissue against a cut on her cheek.

There was, thought Chloe, something vaguely familiar about her, although she couldn't place her as one of the health centre patients. Not surprisingly, she looked apprehensive.

Chloe smiled reassuringly. 'Hello,' she said, 'I'm

Sister Lucas. What's your name, and how can I help you?'

'I'm Jemima,' said the girl in a rush, in a small, shaky voice, 'and the doctor said that you would look at my leg. I've twisted my knee, and I've got a cut on my face. He said that the cut wasn't too deep and wouldn't need stitches and that I shouldn't have a scar. . .and I won't, will I?' Her eyes were huge and pleading in her pale, heart-shaped face. She looked very young and vulnerable, and clearly the thought of being left with a scar was more frightening than anything else at that moment.

'Well, sit down and let me have a look,' said Chloe calmly. Carefully she examined the cut on the girl's cheek just below her right eye. As Dr Meadows had said, it was not deep, but it was nearly twenty-five millimetres long, and would need careful attention if the child was not to be left with a scar. She said gently, 'With luck you won't have a scar after a few months, or only a very faint one, like a hairline, that can be easily disguised. As Dr Meadows said, you don't need stitches. I'll pull the edges of the cut together with narrow strips of plaster, keeping the surfaces perfectly aligned—that should do the trick.'

'Oh, thank you, I should hate to have a scar on my face, and my mother would hate it too.'

'Your mother will be only too glad that you haven't suffered worse injuries,' said Chloe as she worked with painstaking care on the girl's flawless face, with its creamy complexion. 'As long as you're all right, she won't care a bean about scars or anything else.' At last she stood back and looked at her work, and gave a satisfied nod. 'Now that's done, I'll just cover it with a dry dressing, and then see to your leg. We'll put some analgesic cream and a support bandage on that twisted knee.'

'Thank you, Sister,' Jemima said a few minutes later when Chloe had finished attending to her swollen and painful knee. 'That's much better.' She gave a tremulous smile and said, sounding very young and unsure of herself, 'May I go now, please?'

'Not until I've taken a few details and arranged for someone to collect you and take you home. Do you live locally?'

A strange expression crossed Jemima's face, and then her eyes filled with tears. 'No, I don't, but my father does, but he doesn't know that I'm coming to see him. You see. . .' She hesitated, her eyes searching Chloe's face. Chloe smiled and put an arm round her shoulders, as Jemima said in a hesitant whisper, 'Please don't get at me, but I've run away from school.'

Chloe squeezed the girl's shoulder gently. 'And where's school?' she asked in a commendably cool voice, though her mind was racing. That's all they needed to round off the day, an unhappy child absconding from school, with furious parents and school authorities ready to pounce.

'It's a convent school—St Mary's, at Mereshott in Surrey. It only takes an hour to get here on the train, and they won't have missed me yet. Sister Mary Anthony, our headmistress, thinks that I'm having tea with a day girl, as it's near the end of term.'

'When do you break up?'

'The day after tomorrow. My mother was going to collect me, but then I decided to run away, and I was going to ring her from Daddy's house and say that I wanted to stay with him. Only I don't suppose he would have let me.'

'Why wouldn't he?'

'Because he always tries to do the right thing—he wants the courts to let him have custody of me.'

'So your parents are separated?'

'Yes, they're divorced, but I live with my mother, though Daddy's got access to me at any time, only Mummy doesn't like it even though sometimes I'm a nuisance to her when she wants to go out, and Daddy's always busy, though he loves me very much.'

'I'm sure he does, and your mother loves you too.' Chloe's warm heart went out to the child. What a sad state to be in, caught between two bickering adults and longing for the affection of both. But however much she might feel for Jemima she had to act in the child's best interest now. She said firmly, but kindly, 'Well, love, the best thing you can do at this moment is to give me your full name and the phone number of your school, so that I can let them know that you are safe. Then, since your father lives locally, I'll have his address and phone number, and ask him to come and fetch you. What happens after that, I'm afraid, rests with your parents. Now tell me, how old are you, Jemima?'

'I'm thirteen.'

'And your full name is?'

'Jemima Elizabeth Masters.'

Chloe's hand froze over the clipboard. She swallowed, and felt the blood come and go in her face. No wonder the girl had looked familiar with her high cheekbones and cool, grey eyes. There could be no mistaking the likeness to Ben. After a moment she said quietly, 'Is your father Dr Ben Masters?'

'Yes, do you know him?'

'He's a colleague at the health centre; we work together.' Somehow she kept her voice calm, though a mixture of emotions raged within her and a confusion of thoughts whizzed through her mind.

Why on earth had Ben been so secretive about having a daughter? What was wrong with that? And surely it was commendable that he was trying to get custody of her, in spite of being 'a very busy man', as Jemima had described him. Perhaps it was on account of his ex-wife that he was reluctant to talk about his past. She certainly did not sound very motherly, though she had custody of her daughter. Jemima seemed not exactly frightened of her, but awed and anxious to do the right thing by her. Quite clearly she loved her father, and knew that he loved her, whereas she seemed a little uncertain about her mother's affection.

Firmly Chloe thrust all these thoughts aside, as Jemima said eagerly, 'Well, if you work together, you'll know how to get hold of him, won't you?'

'Well, I would normally, but I can't at this moment. He is at the crash site, helping with the injured—it'll be a while before we can contact him. Meanwhile we must let your school know that you are safe.'

'Must you? They'll have to tell my mother and she'll be so angry.'

'I'm sorry, but there's no alternative. And I'm sure she won't be cross—she'll be relieved that you're not badly hurt. But the school has to be told. We'll use the phone in Matron's office, which she has put at our disposal. Come with me.' This isn't real, she thought, as she led the way through the noisy, milling crowd in the reception hall. I've got Ben's daughter in tow.

Suddenly Jemima caught Chloe's sleeve and pulled her to a halt. 'Look, there's Daddy!' she said excitedly, pointing towards the front door. And there, towering above everybody else in the packed room, stood Ben.

'Stay here,' said Chloe quietly. 'Let me go and speak to him first and warn him that you were involved in the accident. He will see that you've been hurt. We don't want to shock him.'

'Oh, I didn't think of that,' replied Jemima, making herself small against the wall, behind a group of people.

Chloe, heart thumping madly at the sight of him, and with anticipation of what she had to tell him, made her way round the groups of chattering people towards Ben, who was still standing by the front door. He saw her when she was almost upon him, and stepped forward, hands outstretched to greet her. He smiled down at her, though his face was drawn with weariness. His fine grey eyes, large and luminous, were warm and compassionate above his aquiline nose and high, strongly moulded cheekbones, as they stared into hers. His likeness to Jemima at that moment was striking.

Chloe's hands trembled as she put them into his. He squeezed them tightly. 'By God, it's good to see you,' he said huskily. 'After all that carnage on the bypass, the last few injured are just being taken away. I thought I'd come and see how you're getting on here. You look pretty busy. Can I do anything to help?'

'No.' Chloe shook her head. 'You've done enough for one day, and we're well organised.' She gave him a rather uncertain smile, and said softly, 'Ben, I'm so glad that you're back, but I've got some news for you, and you must prepare yourself for something of a shock.'

'A shock! What do you mean?' he asked in a surprised voice, and added anxiously, 'You're all right, aren't you; you're not hurt or anything?'

'No, I'm fine,' Chloe assured him. 'It's to do with your daughter, Jemima.'

'Jemima,' he said in an astonished voice. 'What the hell do you know about Jemima?' He stared down at her incredulously.

'She's here, Ben, one of the walking wounded, not seriously hurt. She was on her way to see you when the bus from the station got involved in the pile-up.'

Ben dropped her hands. 'Jemima here—where?' he asked in a staccato voice as he peered over the heads of the milling throng.

'Over there.' Chloe pointed to where she had left the girl. 'Don't be cross with her, Ben,' she said, as he started to push through the crowd towards his daughter. 'She only wanted to see you. . .'

But Ben didn't seem to hear. He had reached Jemima and folded her in his arms. It was quite clear that he wasn't angry with her. He was just relieved to find her in one piece.

Over the top of Jemima's head, in that crowded room, his eyes met Chloe's. As she came closer, he murmured, 'Thank God she isn't badly hurt.'

'Yes, it might have been so much worse.'

They stared at each other, remembering the horrors they had seen that afternoon.

Jemima, snuggled against her father's chest, said in a small, scared voice, 'Daddy, I ran away from school to see you. We were just going to phone to let them know that I'm all right.'

Ben said quietly, 'It's all right, poppet. Don't worry, I'll take care of everything, phone calls and so on. But all I want to do at this moment is to get you home to Poynters.'

'But you're only just moving in—how will you manage?' Chloe asked.

'That's no problem, I'll fix up a bed in one of the spare rooms. I'm quite capable.'

'Oh, I'm sure you are,' said Chloe, feeling strangely deflated, in some vague way wishing that he might need her help, wanting to restore the intimacy that had existed between them earlier in the day. 'I'll make a note on the record that Jemima has been released into your care at your home address.'

'Thank you.' His eyes held hers, grey and steady and full of compassion, understanding—love even. . .? She couldn't be sure. It was as if he had read her vague thoughts.

He said quietly, 'Chloe, if you finish here early enough this evening, come and see me. There's so much that I want to explain to you about this one—' he gave Jemima an extra hug '—and other things.'

She thrilled at the prospect, but forced herself to say, 'But won't Jemima want you to herself tonight?'

'No, she'll be having an early night. She needs to sleep and get over the shock of the accident,' he said, dropping a kiss on Jemima's head. 'Tomorrow we'll talk and sort out our problems, won't we, love?'

'Yes,' said Jemima, giving Chloe a shy smile. 'We can talk tomorrow.'

'Well, if you're sure, I'd love to come.'

'Good, then, duty permitting, I'll see you later.'

Ben smiled at her and dropped another kiss on Jemima's dark head. 'Come on, love,' he said, 'let's go home.' And, keeping a protective arm round her, he steered her through the crowded room and out through the front door.

CHAPTER SEVEN

BY EIGHT o'clock the cottage hospital had returned to
something like normal. All the walking wounded connected with the accident had been treated and sent on
their way, or had been collected by concerned
relatives.

Tired, but in a curious way elated by having done a
good job, Chloe and the other helpers dispersed into
what was now a fine, dry evening. Old Dr Meadows
offered to give Chloe a lift, and dropped her off at
River's End a little before eight-thirty.

Her clothes were bedraggled and filthy after the
day's activities, and her honey-blonde hair a sodden
mass beneath her yachting cap. She still felt shocked
and saddened by what she had seen that afternoon,
but the knowledge that she and Ben had done all they
could for the accident victims raised her spirits somewhat. She was buoyed up, too, by the thought that
she would soon be seeing him, and that of his own
volition he was going to take her into his confidence
concerning Jemima.

She showered, and shampooed her hair, brushing it
until it shone, and left it to swing in a long, loose bob.
She slipped into a sleeveless silk shift dress of a green
that matched her eyes, put on a little light make-up
and a spray of her favourite perfume, and felt ready
for her meeting with Ben.

Suddenly, her tummy churned at the prospect. What
was he going to say to her? Her thoughts flew back to

the morning and the wonderful sensation of being held in his arms. If they had not been interrupted, and they had become emotionally involved, would he have revealed his past to her, or was he only now going to do so because she had inadvertently met Jemima, and his hand had virtually been forced?

No, Ben wouldn't deceive her if he meant their friendship to develop; he was too fine a person for that. In any case it would have been too early to exchange confidences. After all, this morning's incident, the near kiss, had been unexpected and spontaneous, possibly the beginning of something more serious, but who could tell? Only their involvement in the accident this afternoon had charged the situation with a sense of importance.

Feeling rather heavy-hearted, she let herself out of *Luciana* into the warm, scented calm of a perfect July evening and the glowing orange and red of a radiant sunset in a clear, aquamarine sky. The tumultuous rain and wind which had persisted all day and made life so miserable for the injured and the workers at the scene of the accident had given way to this beautiful evening.

She picked her way carefully, in her strappy sandals, along the cinder path to Poynters. And then, as she had that morning, she walked up the garden path to the kitchen door. But this time there was no need to ring the bell; Ben was in the kitchen waiting for her.

He flung the door wide and smiled, a wholly welcoming smile. Her heart lifted. She smiled back at him.

He put out his hands and drew her into the kitchen. 'Chloe, I'm so glad that you could make it.' His eyes swept over her. 'You look lovely,' he said softly.

'Rather different from when I last saw you.' Then he looked down at her bare brown sandalled feet, and his smile broadened.

'What, no wellies?' he asked.

'Not this evening. In case you hadn't noticed, it's stopped raining and there's a beautiful sunset, and the towpath's drained nicely.' And I'm babbling too much, she thought, because he's touching me. She asked quickly, to bring herself back to earth, 'Where's Jemima?'

'Asleep, as I told you she would be. She's worn out, poor child, what with the accident and her personal problems. Thank you for looking after her so well and reassuring her about not being severely scarred. That's all she seems to be worried about, whereas I'm just grateful that her injury wasn't any nearer her eye. There might have been a real problem had it been an inch or so higher.'

'Yes, it might. I'm so glad it wasn't worse.'

Only the ticking of the wall-clock broke the silence as they smiled into each other's eyes, caught in some magic bond. Ben tightened his hold on her hands. He looked down at her, his eyes, with a network of tired lines around them, full of warmth. How could she ever have thought them cold and flinty!

'Oh, Chloe,' he said huskily, 'what a hell of a day it's been.' He drew her unresisting into his arms. She rested her head against his chest and heard the steady beating of his heart. He kissed the crown of her shining head, but it was a kiss of compassion rather than passion. He needed comfort, and wanted to give comfort after the trauma of the day. She was safe in his arms.

They clung together for several minutes as love and

tenderness flowed between them, letting some of the pain and the suffering they had witnessed that day drain away, until at last he said, loosening his hold on her, 'Poor love, you must be starving, I've prepared a supper of sorts. Come and eat.' He steered her toward the long refectory table that graced the centre of the room, and sat her down in a ladder-back chair.

'I hope you don't mind eating in the kitchen?' he asked, busying himself at the Aga.

'Not at all. It's the hub, the heart of the house.'

Ben gave a quirky grin. 'Well, you should know, you spent enough time in it this morning, unpacking and so on.'

'This morning seems a world away.'

'Indeed, a world away. Such waste, all those dead and injured.' His voice was bitter, and she saw that his face was sad; and then his expression changed and a smile tugged at his lips, and he said softly, 'But you know, Chloe love, there was a moment in the midst of all that carnage that for me was special. I'm not over-sentimental, but I must say that when you held the baby Fiona in your arms, looking the perfect mother, I was much moved. Remember?'

Remember! Of course she did. She remembered how he had looked at her, and the way he had said, 'As her own,'—at first to reassure the injured Diana, and then repeated for her alone. Chloe's heart lurched. Surely he couldn't know how she had felt, holding the sleeping infant. With all his perceptiveness, he couldn't read her mind, couldn't know how small babies affected her, were a constant reminder that it was likely she was going to remain childless. There was no need for him to know, not yet, perhaps not ever.

A small wave of panic washed over her. She forced herself to give him a bright smile. 'How fanciful,' she said with a brittle little laugh. 'And I thought that I was just being a good nurse.'

For an instant Ben showed his surprise at her manner and his strongly marked eyebrows came together in a frown. Then his frown cleared and he said softly, 'Well, of course you were being a good nurse, but you were also being a woman.' He paused for a moment, his grey eyes dark with emotion as he surveyed her across the room. Then he smiled. 'Now let's eat. Just tinned soup, I'm afraid, gingered up with sherry, and rolls and cheese, with fruit to follow, and coffee by the litre. It'll keep body and soul together.'

'It sounds wonderful.'

'Then tuck in and enjoy it, please.'

'I will.'

They didn't talk much as they ate. They were both hungry, both tired, both emotionally overwhelmed by the situation, and yet, in spite of everything, in a curious way at ease with one another. It was an odd sensation.

Chloe finished peeling a peach, and said eventually, to break the silence that embraced them, 'Presumably you had no difficulty contacting the school and Jemima's mother to explain the situation.'

'The school was no problem. I had a long chat with the headmistress and got things straightened out, but had to leave a message on Ursula's answerphone as she was out. I hope to hear back from her shortly.'

'She will be relieved to know that Jemima is safe and sound and with you.'

'To know that she is relatively unhurt, yes, but not

that she is with me, I'm afraid,' he said matter-of-factly, confirming what Jemima had told Chloe that afternoon about her mother disliking her being with her father.

'I'm so sorry, Ben. Jemima implied as much, but she was distressed and I hoped that she might be exaggerating.'

Ben stared at her for a moment with unseeing eyes, his ruggedly handsome face looking troubled. He pushed back his chair noisily. 'I need a drink,' he said. 'If you've finished eating, let's go into the sitting-room. It's reasonably tidy and we can be more comfortable there while we talk.' He came round the table, took hold of her hand and pulled her to her feet. 'Come on.' He gave her a wry smile. 'I said that I would come clean about my private life, and I will.'

'You don't have to,' she said, as he led her across the spacious hall.

'Oh, yes, I do, my dear Chloe, if our relationship is to progress, and my intuition tells me that we both want it to. And, that being so, there must be no secrets between us.'

She breathed in sharply and came to a halt in the middle of the hall, pulling him to a standstill. His frankness startled her. He turned and faced her. Chloe looked hard at him, studying every detail of his face, from his square jutting chin to his expressive grey eyes and widow's peak of grey-streaked black hair. 'What do you mean,' she said breathlessly, 'your *intuition*, a *relationship*? I thought only women had intuition, and we've hardly known each other long enough to have a relationship.'

He returned her gaze steadily and said in a deep, gravelly voice, 'What does time matter, when two people are drawn together as we are? And women haven't the monopoly on intuition, you know; any good doctor will tell you that.' He took a step towards her, dropped the hand he had been leading her by and put both his hands on her shoulders. 'Chloe, I want to tell you about my failed marriage, be totally honest with you. I want this *relationship*, or whatever you choose to call it, to get off to a clean start. You're still a young and beautiful woman, with lots of friends, but I suspect that you are lonely at times. We both know what it's like to be bereft of love, do we not? Your marriage was brought to a sudden end by accident, mine drifted into meaninglessness. We're both naturally reserved where our emotions are concerned, and we're both workaholics. But work isn't everything—we need other things in life. Above all, we need love, Chloe. And I think that's what we've got to offer each other.'

'L. . .love,' she faltered, her heart hammering in her ears. To hear him admit to the emotion was a shock. As yet it was something she hardly dared admit to herself, and yet here he was, using the word boldly.

'Love,' he confirmed. 'I see no virtue in pretending otherwise; it's been there in the air since we first met, has it not?'

This can't be happening to me, thought Chloe, this reserved, rather remote man, speaking of love. True, the events of the day had almost dragged them together, underlined their attraction for each other, but to speak seriously of love!

There was a deadly hush in the hall. Involuntarily Chloe looked toward the stairs. 'Jemima,' she whispered, very conscious of the child's presence in the house.

'Still sound asleep,' he said softly, and then added with a teasing, quiet chuckle that made him suddenly look and sound years younger, 'I promise we won't disturb her. I'm not suggesting an orgy of wild love-making tonight, you know, just a chance to explain myself and put the record straight before we proceed further. I'm determined this time around that there won't be any mistakes, which is why I want to fill you in on my murky past. So let's talk, Chloe, now.'

She tried to suppress her racing pulse and whirling thoughts, and be as controlled as he seemed to be. 'Of course.' Somehow she raised a smile of sorts, and said calmly, 'Let's talk.'

He bent forward, thrilling her as he touched her lips lightly with his, then led her into the sitting-room.

It was dark now, and he switched on wall-lights, flooding the long, low room that stretched from front to back of the house with a soft amber light. It was a lovely room, both homely and gracious. The polished wooden floor, with its scattering of pale Chinese rugs, glowed in the lamplight. Chintz-covered armchairs and occasional tables were dotted about the room. Facing the elegant Adam fireplace was a large, cream-coloured, soft leather sofa. Old gold velvet curtains framed the large windows at each end of the room. Except for the empty bookshelves on either side of the fireplace, bare walls and a few packing-cases stacked neatly in a corner, the room already looked lived in.

In spite of the chaotic thoughts chasing round in her head, blotting out practically everything else, Chloe was struck by the beauty and serenity of the room, and commented, 'It's lovely. How on earth have you managed to get it tidied so quickly? No one would believe that you only moved in this morning.'

Ben said with a smile, 'Well, I must admit to having help. Mrs Alcot, one of my patients, has agreed to come to me as housekeeper. She has a key and let herself in this afternoon while you and I were knee-deep in the carnage on the bypass. She has worked wonders. I believe she is going to turn out to be a real treasure, as they say.'

'Yes, I know Mrs Alcot, and she certainly will be invaluable to you. You're lucky to have her, since she has only recently been widowed.'

'So I understand. But she seems very keen to get going and work off some of her grief. I think we'll be good for each other.' He pushed Chloe gently into a corner of the sofa, and said, pulling a face, 'Now let's forget Mrs Alcot, treasure though she may be, and concentrate on us. I think we are making conversation for the sake of it, don't you?'

'Yes, I'm afraid we are.'

They exchanged gentle, wry smiles of complete understanding.

Ben said, 'I won't prevaricate any longer, but before I start, what'll you have to drink?'

'A brandy please, to round off that delicious meal.'

He gave a crack of laughter. 'Well, it wasn't exactly cordon bleu but it filled the gap. I'll join you in the brandy.' He moved over to a side-table laden with bottles, and poured their drinks.

He handed Chloe hers and then sat himself down at the other end of the sofa, took a sip of brandy, swirled the golden liquid around in his glass, and stared at it. 'Where to begin,' he said quietly, 'without boring you to death?'

'Oh, Ben, you know you can never do that. I want to know all there is to know about you and, since this afternoon, about Jemima too.'

'Jemima.' Ben's austere face softened. 'She was the best thing that ever came out of my marriage. Sadly, Ursula didn't think so. She was furious when she discovered that she was pregnant. Talked of having a termination but, thank goodness, couldn't quite see that through.'

Chloe felt her stomach knot up at the idea that someone who could have a child didn't want one, when she. . . Best not go down that line of thought.

'Didn't you know that she didn't want children?'

'No, we never discussed it. To be fair to Ursula, it might not have made any difference had I known how she felt. I was besotted with her at the time. She was eighteen, a flawless, beautiful girl. Men swarmed round her. I was twenty-four. Her parents encouraged the match, mine didn't, but I was in no mood to listen to them. I had some money of my own as well as what I could earn in medicine, and could comfortably support a wife. It was a whirlwind romance; we were married in a few weeks. But I'm afraid the old proverb was true about marrying in haste and repenting at leisure. Things started to go wrong from the time she knew she was pregnant, whereas I was thrilled at the idea of having a child.'

He stared down at his glass, looking infinitely sad.

Chloe said softly, 'Oh, Ben, I'm so sorry. Life must have been hell for you.' She stretched out a hand and he took it, holding it loosely in his long, lean fingers.

'It was pretty grim for both of us most of the time, just staying together. But there was no question of our parting once I knew that she was pregnant. And

Ursula's people, with whom I got on extremely well, were very wealthy and they threatened to disinherit her if we separated. Ursula couldn't contemplate a future without their sort of money, so stayed with me.'

'But you are divorced now.'

'Yes. Sadly, her parents were killed in an air crash two years ago, and she inherited everything, so there was no obstacle from her point of view to our getting divorced. I agreed for Jemima's sake; I felt that she was suffering because of our total incompatibility. But I was devastated at having to hand over custody of her.' His voice, which had been low and soft, hardened. 'But that I hope one day to remedy,' he added fiercely. He looked very determined and squeezed Chloe's hand hard. 'Ursula might yet be persuaded to hand her over to me without too much trouble, in order to get on with her own social life. I hope that may be the case and we can settle without too much acrimony. But at least the courts may be more inclined in my favour now that I have a family house and full-time domestic help to back me up. Previously they wouldn't consider me, a busy doctor living in a bachelor flat, having custody. But now I'm going to fight for my daughter. She's unhappy with her mother, especially now that Ursula is considering marriage to someone whom Jemima dislikes intensely.'

'Why on earth does Ursula want to keep custody of Jemima, if she finds her such a drag?'

Ben released her hand and laced his fingers round the bowl of his glass. He said thoughtfully, 'Partly because in her own way she loves her, partly because it's expected of her to play the part of a good mother, and partly to prevent me having Jemima.'

'How could she be so spiteful? It's wicked to use the child for such reasons.'

'Spiteful, yes, which is why I'm normally meticulous about seeing Jemima. Today, of course, is different. Generally I see her only when an outing has been agreed.' He put down his glass and turned to Chloe. 'Well, there's the end of the saga where my daughter is concerned. It's important that you know how I feel about her. I want to care for her and will do everything in my power to——'

He was interrupted by the ringing of the doorbell, a long ring, followed by several staccato short ones.

A curious expression passed over his face, and he ground out in a low, hard voice, 'I'd know that ring anywhere, but I just don't believe it. Why the hell couldn't she have phoned before tearing down here?'

It was a rhetorical question and he stared blankly at Chloe as he said it. She stared back, the awful truth beginning to dawn on her as she did so. It was obvious who 'she' was.

The bell was rung again, several short impatient rings.

'I'm afraid,' said Ben in a steely voice, 'that our late visitor is Ursula, my ex-wife. I'd better let her in before she wakes Jemima.' He stood up and looked down at Chloe. His voice softened. 'You know,' he said, 'I wouldn't have had this happen for the world.'

'Well, it has happened, and I'd better go.' Chloe half rose from the sofa.

'No.' With a firm hand to match his voice Ben pushed her back on to the couch. 'Stay there. We will do this in a civilised manner—you're not to go skulking off because my wayward ex-wife decides to visit at an ungodly hour.'

The doorbell pealed again and Ben, muttering beneath his breath, left the room. Feeling stunned, Chloe sat staring into space. Then she heard the murmur of voices and the sound of high heels click-clacking across the parquet floor of the hall. The half closed door of the sitting-room was suddenly thrust wide open to reveal a beautiful woman standing in the doorway. She was petite, about five foot nothing, with a cloud of red-gold hair, a heart-shaped face, and sapphire-blue eyes. Ursula Masters! No wonder Ben had fallen in love with the eighteen-year-old version. She must have been even more lovely then, with youth and innocence on her side.

She came to a halt when she saw Chloe, and then came slowly into the room. 'So you *do* have a visitor,' she said over her shoulder to Ben.

'As I told you,' he replied in clipped tones. 'A friend and colleague, Chloe Lucas.' He gave Chloe a sort of half-bow, and indicated Ursula. 'My ex-wife, Ursula Masters.'

Chloe held out a hand, which after a moment Ursula Masters grasped. 'How do you do?' they said in cautious unison.

Ursula gave a tight smile. 'Well, how young and pretty you are,' she said, and added waspishly, 'How lucky Ben is to have you as a colleague.'

Chloe wished that she had coiled her hair up into her usual sophisticated chignon style, so that she looked years older. She also wished that she were anywhere but in Ben's sitting-room with this rude, sarcastic woman.

Ben said sharply, 'That'll do, Ursula. Stop talking rubbish.'

'Rubbish, Ben! Oh, come on, young women always

have had a penchant for you, and you haven't exactly fought them off, have you?'

'Ursula,' he ground out furiously in his deep voice, his eyes like granite, 'don't say another word, you're embarrassing my guest.'

Heart thudding uncomfortably, Chloe rose to her feet. 'It's all right, Ben, I'm going. You and Mrs Masters have a lot to talk about.'

'Don't rush off on my account, Ms Lucas,' said Ursula. 'I've only come to collect my daughter and then I'll be gone.'

'You can't take Jemima tonight,' Ben said brusquely. 'She's sedated and sleeping heavily. As a doctor, I forbid you to move her.'

'Really? We'll see about that. You can't forbid me to do anything where my daughter's concerned.' Ursula's sapphire eyes flashed, her mouth set in a mutinous line.

Ben said in a cold voice, 'Even you, my dear Ursula, wouldn't do anything so foolish as to move her tonight. Now take a seat and wait while I see my visitor off.' Gently he took Chloe's arm and steered her to the door.

Chloe said politely over her shoulder, 'Goodnight, Mrs Masters.'

'Goodnight,' came the curt reply.

In the kitchen, Ben took Chloe's hands in his. 'I'm so sorry about all of this,' he murmured. 'You should never have been involved. I do apologise for Ursula's comments. She is, I think, much more shocked by Jemima's accident that she realises, and that's why she spoke as she did. Whatever her faults, she's not usually so blatantly rude.'

'It's OK,' said Chloe softly. 'Now I must go and

leave you to sort things out about Jemima. Thank you for being so frank with me earlier this evening, and for the nice things you said. Goodnight, Ben.' She reached up and kissed him on his cheek.

'Goodnight, Chloe love.' He cupped her face in his hands and looked intently down at her, and then brushed her lips with his. 'Thanks for everything today, though I wish parts of it might have been different. I'll ring you tomorrow.'

He opened the door and switched on the garden lights, watching until she disappeared through the gate with a wave of her hand. The garden faded back into darkness as he switched off the lights and returned to the sitting-room and the truculent Ursula.

CHAPTER EIGHT

CHLOE slept badly, her mind full of chaotic thoughts about the horrendous accident, Jemima's unexpected appearance, Ben's confidences, and the totally mind-boggling arrival of Ursula Masters.

What a poisonous person she was, at least where Ben was concerned. All those innuendoes about him and younger women, as if he set out to attract them on purpose. And what about her attitude to Jemima? Was it just spite against Ben that made her want to keep custody, or did she love her daughter in her own peculiar way, and was afraid of losing her completely to Ben? Well, perhaps last night's confrontation between the two of them would produce something positive. And what if it did? How might it affect her own just budding relationship with Ben?

What relationship? They hadn't even kissed properly yet. Yesterday had been like a sick French farce, where every time they were about to get together something happened to keep them apart. Ursula's arrival last night, just after Ben had spoken of love and had been so frank about Jemima and his intentions, had been the last straw in an eventful day. So far, all their infant relationship had produced was a few snatched embraces, some meaningful eye contact, and a deep sense of rapport with each other. But was it enough to build a future on?

He had been completely honest with her about Jemima; should she not be equally honest about her own fear, suppressed for years, that she might be infertile? Was she ready to tell him about that?

With an impatient snort, she threw back the bed-clothes and got out of bed. No use lying around and thinking until her head ached. She must put it all out of her mind. Do something useful. With all her heart she wished that she were on duty. Work was a pana-cea, an antidote to personal anxiety and stress.

Well, there was no reason why she shouldn't go to work. She could take herself off leave. She could at least call in at the health centre and see if all was well, even if she only stayed for a short while. Anything was better than just lounging around and thinking and waiting for Ben to phone. Having reached this decision, she showered quickly, dressed in a cool, lemon-coloured linen suit, and set off through the brilliant morning sunshine for the centre.

Betty Box greeted her warmly. 'Well, you're a sight for sore eyes,' she said with obvious relief. 'You must be psychic or something, coming in when you're most needed. Susan's off—one of her kids has gone down with chickenpox, and she can't get in till her mother arrives this afternoon. And Fee, who would have relieved her on bloods and cervical smears, has badly sprained her wrist and her right thumb and is virtually useless, though she's hanging about willing to do anything that she can cope with. I was just going to ring around off-duty staff to see who would come in. I know you didn't have much of a day off yesterday helping out at the RTA, but now you're here. . .?' She trailed off hopefully.

Thank God for emergencies, thought Chloe, I've got a cast-iron excuse for staying. She smiled at Betty. 'I'll be happy to help out. I wasn't doing anything in

particular. Just give me a moment to change and I'll
have the first patient in.'

On her way to her office she bumped into Geoffrey
Murray just coming out of his consulting-room. The
senior partner looked harassed, but his face lit up
when he saw Chloe.

'What on earth are you doing here?' he asked.
'You're supposed to be on leave. Not,' he added
hastily, 'that I'm not delighted to see you. We've got
a bit of a mini-crisis on.'

'Yes, Betty told me. I'm just going to get changed
and do the bloods and smears.'

Geoffrey looked immensely relieved. 'Sure you
don't mind?'

'Not at all.'

'Then do you think you can fit in another "blood"
on your list? A rather nervous lady I've just been
seeing, a Mrs Turner. She's presenting with all sorts
of symptoms, poor woman, but I certainly think she's
anaemic among other things, and the sooner I have
some answers to her haemoglobin and iron levels, the
better. She also needs an ECG—I think she may have
a mild heart problem. If that could be done as soon as
possible I'd be grateful. I was going to do it myself if
necessary, but with Ben away settling into his new
house, we're short on our side too.'

'Not to worry. I think Fee can cope with the ECG
even with her sprained wrist. Mrs Turner can have
that done first while I get on with some of the booked-
in patients on the list, and then I'll see her a bit later
to do her blood test.'

'Fine, I'll leave it with you, Chloe. She's in the
waiting-room at the moment. And thanks for stepping
into the breach once more,' he said with a smile.

'A pleasure,' said Chloe, continuing her way to her office.

She changed quickly and went through to the clinic-room to find Fiona—Fee—tidying out cupboards with her left hand.

Fee let out a cry of delight. 'Chloe, am I glad to see you! I suppose you've heard all about our problems from Betty.'

'Yes, she's filled me in and I'm going to lend a hand. But tell me, how on earth did you hurt your wrist?'

'Slipped on the stairs and tried to stop myself falling by grabbing at the banisters. Thought I'd fractured it at first, but fortunately it turned out to be just a sprain.'

'Poor old you, but that's just as painful and immobilising.'

'You can say that again. You don't realise how much you depend on two hands until one is virtually useless. If only there were something I could do.'

'Think you could manage an ECG?'

'Oh, rather, I'm sure that I could cope with that. I can put the leads in place with my left hand, and use my right hand a little if necessary.'

'Good.' Chloe passed on the information about Mrs Turner. 'Perhaps, as she's rather nervous, you'd better explain that an electrocardiograph is an instrument to measure her heartbeats and not some form of treatment.'

'Right, I will do. I'll just get myself organised and have the lady in straight away.'

'That's great. Shout out if you get stuck.'

'OK.'

Fee went through to the small treatment-room

which housed a couch and the ECG monitoring machine, and Chloe began preparing her various vials, syringes, needles and forms for blood-taking.

She had a long list of patients to see, and lost no time in getting started. Fortunately, until she got to Mrs Turner, they were all easy to take blood from, with nicely distended veins into which she could smoothly slide a needle.

It was a different picture though with Mrs Turner. She was incredibly nervous and her veins were slack and flaccid, and it took a while to reassure her and take her blood sample. By the time she had finished, Mrs Turner was pale and clammy and on the verge of fainting. Chloe pushed her head between her knees to restore the blood flow to the brain, and then gave her a glucose drink before escorting her back to her husband in the waiting-room. He seemed nearly as nervous as his wife.

'I'll just check with Dr Murray and find out if he's ready to see you again,' Chloe explained as she settled Mrs Turner beside her husband. 'I know he wants to tell you the result of your ECG.'

'Do you think there is anything serious, Sister?' asked Mr Turner anxiously.

'I don't know, Mr Turner,' said Chloe gently. 'But Dr Murray will be able to tell you more and advise the right treatment. He's a splendid doctor; you're in good hands.'

'Oh, we've heard that, but we've only just retired here, you see, so we haven't seen him before. We were so used to our old doctor. It's a bit nerve-racking when you start with someone new.'

What a pity that the Turners' old doctor hadn't done more investigations into Mrs Turner's condition,

Chloe thought, as, moments later, she tapped on the door of Geoffrey's consulting-room. She must have been showing symptoms that something was wrong for a long while.

Geoffrey was examining the read-out strip of Mrs Turner's ECG, and turned to Chloe with a smile. 'Well, I'm happy to say that that's not too bad,' he said. 'She is mildly fibrillating but it should be controllable with medication and rest, and when we get the results of her blood tests hopefully I'll be able to treat whatever's wrong there too without hospitalising her.'

'Oh, I am pleased that it's nothing more serious. The Turners are in quite a state.'

'Well, wheel them in, and I'll tell them the good news.'

'Right.'

After finishing the bloods, Chloe turned to her list for cervical smear tests. There were only five patients to see, and they were all perfectly straightforward cases, though one patient, a sixty-year-old woman, showed signs of a prolapsed uterus. Chloe advised her to make an appointment to see Dr Alison Knight, her practice doctor, in the near future, to confirm whether a repair to the uterus or a hysterectomy was indicated.

That it was suddenly lunchtime came as a surprise, and Chloe was happy and relieved to find that she had been too busy to think about Ben or her personal problems all morning. Now, though, they returned in full force. Ben had asked if he might ring her. Had he rung already? she wondered with a quickening heart-beat. Would he have been disappointed because she wasn't there? Would he want to see her today; would he have the chance? Had the beautiful, wilful Ursula stayed the night at Poynters? Suddenly she wanted the answers to all these questions. She wanted to get back to River's End and news from Ben.

'Come and eat with us,' invited Betty and Fee. 'Our treat, since you came to the rescue this morning.'

'No, thanks, I want to get back home and restart my little holiday. Bye for now—see you later in the week.'

It was cooler by the river than in the middle of town, and the tall poplars that fringed the Chid shaded *Luciana* and the other houseboats moored along the banks. It was also soothingly quiet at this time of the day, with only the occasional walker on the towpath and nothing and nobody stirring on the water. Everyone appeared to be at lunch or having a siesta, Chloe thought as she parked her car. Which was what she was going to do, she decided as she went on board: eat and sleep. The tubbed roses and honeysuckle that twined round the wooden fencing of the front porch gave off a delicate scent in the midday heat. She sniffed appreciatively as she let herself into the saloon.

Home—what could be nicer, especially now that she had worked herself into a deliciously happy state of mind? The uncertainty with which she had started the day seemed to have vanished. Her emotions, which had gone up and down like a roller-coaster in the early hours of the morning, now seemed on an even keel. She was looking forward to a quiet afternoon and Ben's phone call.

She discovered that she was ravenously hungry and, after changing into an ancient pair of shorts and a loose sleeveless top, she made her way to the narrow little galley kitchen to make herself a sandwich. She had just cut two slices of wholemeal bread when there was a loud, insistent knocking at her front door.

Who on earth could it be? The postman perhaps? She couldn't think of anyone else—her neighbours were either away on holiday or at work.

Unless. . . Could it possibly be Ben? Had he come to see her instead of telephoning? Her heart rocked madly at the possibility as she made her way to the door, and all sorts of silly thoughts rushed through her head. What would they say to each other after the awkwardness of last night? Would he kiss her? She wished that she hadn't changed into old shorts. The lemon-coloured suit she had worn that morning was much more feminine.

She took a few deep breaths to calm herself. She mustn't give away her feelings too obviously—play it cool. She pinned an impersonal, welcoming smile on her face, and opened the door.

Ursula Masters stood on her doorstep!

For a moment the two women stared at each other in silence, Chloe with her smile frozen on her lips in surprise, while Ursula's almost too perfect face remained expressionless.

Somehow Chloe pulled herself together, squashed her amazement at the sight of her visitor, and said in a quiet voice, 'Good afternoon, Mrs Masters. This is a surprise. I thought that you'd gone back to London. Do come in.' She opened the door wide and stood aside.

'I decided to stay over last night to discuss Jemima and other matters with Ben,' said Ursula airily, as she passed Chloe and entered the roomy saloon-cum-sitting-room. She looked around her with open curiosity, her finely plucked eyebrows raised expressively, apparently surprised by what she saw. 'This is rather attractive in an arty sort of way,' she said in a condescending manner. She smiled slightly. 'I must say I had no idea that a houseboat could be so——' she hesitated '—so comfortable and so well appointed. One somehow thinks of houseboats as being on a par with caravans and travellers and such like.'

She might as well have said the great unwashed, the rude bitch, thought Chloe, suppressing a swell of anger. 'There are houseboats and houseboats,' she said evenly, 'just as there are caravans and caravans. We're lucky here, being moored in such a super place.'

'Yes, you are. Very upmarket.'

'Yes,' Chloe said tersely, fighting to keep control of her temper. Apparently the petite, faultlessly turned out woman standing in front of her was quite unaware that she was being offensive. How on earth had Ben fallen in love with such a creature? She might look flawless on the outside, but her crass indifference to other people's feelings was appalling. Had she perhaps been different when she was younger? Not likely. Then she must have been like a spoiled child, pouting prettily and helplessly until she got her own way. Perhaps that was what had attracted him, her helplessness as well as her beauty. He would have wanted to protect her. Sharply she dismissed her racing thoughts, and said coolly, 'Do sit down, Mrs Masters, and tell me why you have come to see me.'

Her visitor looked at her in some surprise. 'Can't you guess?' she asked.

'No, of course not, how could I? I haven't a clue. We've only just met; I don't know you. I can't think what we have to talk about.'

'Well, obviously, about you and Ben,' Ursula Masters said bluntly.

'About Ben and me!' said Chloe in utter astonishment. She felt her cheeks redden and then go pale. What on earth did the woman mean? Surely Ben hadn't discussed her with his ex-wife? 'But there's nothing to say about us,' she said in a steady, firm voice. 'We work together, we're just colleagues——'

'I know,' interrupted Ursula with a theatrical sigh. 'You're just good friends. But that's nonsense and you and I both know it. I could sense the atmosphere when I arrived last night. And I know Ben. He's attracted to you all right, but that's largely because you're exactly the sort of woman he's looking for; you fit the bill perfectly from his point of view. You're a young, pretty, caring, professional woman—what could be more suitable for the role he has in mind for you?'

Common sense told Chloe that she ought to stop this ridiculous conversation before it got out of hand. A shiver of apprehension went through her, but her curiosity and temper were aroused by Ursula Masters' whole tone and manner, and she asked in a voice throbbing with anger, 'What on earth do you mean by that peculiar remark?'

Her visitor's lips curled into a disdainful smile. 'You really haven't got his measure yet, have you?' she said. 'Can't you see? Isn't it obvious that you would make an ideal proxy mother to present to the powers-that-be, when he tries to get custody of Jemima? Any court would look more favourably on a father suitably married or about to be married to a woman like yourself. No wonder he's allowed himself to fall in love with you.'

Mesmerised by her sheer audacity, Chloe stared in disbelief at Ursula Masters. She couldn't be hearing right. How could the woman say such things? Allowed himself! Looked upon her as a proxy mother! As if Ben would use her like that. He was falling in love with her for her own sake, he'd said as much last night, hadn't he? But was he deluding himself? A flutter of uncertainty went through her. Could there be any truth in what this poisonous, spiteful creature was saying? Could this woman who didn't want Ben for herself, but wouldn't allow anyone else to have him, be right? Or was she muddying the waters to make it more difficult for Ben to get custody of Jemima? Did she really think that if Ben were married it would enhance his chances and was therefore doing everything in her power to prevent it?

One thing was clear; she mustn't listen to any more of this nonsense. It was disloyal to Ben and agony for herself to hear such things said of him.

She took a deep breath, and said calmly, 'Mrs Masters, I think you had better go.'

Ursula Masters' face twisted into a sardonic smile. 'Don't you want to know any more about our precious Ben?' she asked in a hard voice.

'No, thank you, you've said enough. I'll leave Ben to tell me anything more of his own volition.'

'Well, of course he won't admit to wanting to marry you for Jemima's sake, but be warned, that's his true motive. He would do anything to gain custody.'

With difficulty, Chloe held her tongue and her temper in check. She moved across the saloon and opened the front door. 'Please go, Mrs Masters,' she said in a flat, frosty voice.

* * *

For some minutes after Ursula Masters had gone Chloe stood with her back to the front door staring into space, mind seething, body shaking. She felt raw, violated, in shock. Nobody had ever spoken to her like that before. Like an automaton she moved to the kitchen and made herself a cup of coffee and took it into the sitting-room. She sipped it while it was scalding hot, and after a while began to get her thoughts straightened out.

It was hard to believe that the conversation she had had with Ben's ex-wife really had taken place, hard to believe that she had been here at all. But she had; her expensive perfume still lingered in the air. The woman's audacity was breathtaking. How had she dared to say such palpably untrue things to someone whom she scarcely knew?

It was obvious. She had dared because she was determined to keep custody of Jemima and hurt Ben as much as she could. She would do or say anything to that end. As Chloe began to think more clearly, she realised that she must try to ignore what the woman had said as a load of dangerous nonsense uttered out of vindictiveness.

For of course there couldn't possibly be any truth in what she had said, could there?

The silent question seemed to hang in the air. Chloe held her breath for a moment and then shook her head. 'No, of course there isn't,' she murmured out loud. 'No truth at all.'

Of course there wasn't! She mustn't even begin to doubt Ben's motives for wanting to pursue their relationship—that was precisely what his ex-wife wanted, for her to doubt. So he might be in a stronger position to seek custody if he was married. Well, that

might be true. But they were only just at the beginning
of any sort of meaningful friendship, and marriage at
this moment didn't come into it.

The suggestions that Ursula had made haunted her.
Impatiently she washed up her coffee-cup and made a
half-hearted attempt to finish making the sandwich
she had started, but abandoned it because she no
longer felt hungry. Some obscure need to keep busy
with her hands made her decide to do some baking.

In spite of her determination not to doubt Ben, all
the time she was working, unpalatable thoughts continued to swirl around in her mind, triggered off by
Ursula's innuendoes. He wouldn't deliberately mis-
lead her, but supposing subconsciously he was trying
to put himself in a stronger position to get custody of
Jemima? Wouldn't he do exactly as Ursula suggested
and make a suitable marriage? Well, if this was the
case, did it mean that he would necessarily love her
any the less? Did he love her? He had used the word
'love' yesterday evening—had he meant it?

She was automatically rubbing fat into flour, her
mind working overtime, when there was a knock at
the door. She glanced at the wall-clock; it was after
four. This time it probably was a neighbour returned
from work, come for a cup of tea and a chat. Chloe
sighed. She could have done without either at this
moment; she wanted to be alone with her thoughts.

Rinsing her hands under the tap, she dried them as
she went to the door.

There was a second knock. She reached the door,
flung it wide open and found Ben standing in the
porch. He looked very angry, his lean, rugged face
grim and unsmiling.

For the second time that afternoon, she was almost

speechless. Earlier in the day, she had half thought that he might call, but now, after Ursula's visit, he was the last person she expected to see.

The look on his face was daunting. Her heart seemed to stand still.

'B. . . Ben,' she said. 'What's wrong?'

'Ursula's been here, right?' he said in a low, tightly controlled voice, his eyes boring into hers.

Chloe forced herself to meet his flinty stare unflinchingly. 'Why, yes, she was here, but I didn't exactly invite her. I don't even know how she knew where to find me.' Amazingly she kept her voice steady.

'Apparently she saw you come home from an upstairs window and decided to visit you—girl talk, she called it. She's gone back to London now. Her parting shot was that she had put you in the picture about me and my intentions. Sounded very cosy.' His voice was full of irony.

Anger and disappointment swamped her. He was almost accusing her of conspiring with his rotten ex-wife. How could he?

A party of walkers was coming along the towpath.

'You'd better come in,' she said sharply, pressing herself against the wall to allow him to pass through the narrow archway leading to the saloon. 'We can't have a slanging match out here.'

'Have no fear, I don't go in for slanging matches,' he grated in an icy-cold voice that sent a shiver down her spine. 'But I have come to find out what slanderous remarks Ursula has been making about me and with what nonsense she's been filling your innocent head.' He looked grim and determined.

They stood facing each other in the middle of the room. The word 'innocent' infuriated her. Somehow he made it sound as if she was an empty-headed, gullible girl instead of a sensible, intelligent woman.

She drew herself up to her full height and said with dignity, 'Mrs Masters didn't fill my head with anything. Certainly we talked about you and Jemima, and she made some interesting and not always kind observations, but that was all. She said nothing that I wasn't capable of dealing with.'

His eyes flashed angrily as he looked down at her.

'For God's sake, woman,' he said roughly. 'You're no match for the Ursulas of this world; you're too honest. I know how clever she is with words, the planting of ideas, the innuendoes she will have made about my integrity. Use your common sense and put everything she said out of your mind.'

Chloe felt the blood rush into her cheeks. He was right, of course, Ursula had behaved as he said, but how dared he practically order her to ignore his ex-wife's words?

Unable to lie directly to him, but smarting at his arrogant attitude, she said spiritedly, 'Of course I didn't believe everything she told me, but some things made sense of a kind, and I've got to think it through, and I shall take my own time doing so.' She lifted her head defiantly, and looked him straight in the eye.

He stared back, a small, cold smile playing round his mouth. 'Really? So you would take her word rather than mine? I hoped better of you than that.' He gave Chloe a penetrating, thoughtful look as if he were turning something over in his mind, then shook his head slowly. 'My God,' he said bitterly, 'you think I *am* interested in you primarily to give me a stronger hand where Jemima is concerned, don't you? That's the nonsense that Ursula fed you. And you believed her. . .' A strange look passed over his face.

In spite of the heat, Chloe felt cold. He was very angry. His face and body were taut with temper and controlled rage. What had she done by being so proud and outspoken? Why hadn't she instead attempted to discuss with him what Ursula had implied? He was far too perceptive and, knowing his ex-wife as he did, had guessed what had been said anyway, and was furious with her for even considering that there might be some truth in it. If she had approached him in a different manner they might have resolved the matter.

'I didn't say that I believed her,' she said in a small voice.

'No, but she succeeded in sowing some seeds of doubt, did she not?' His voice was full of contempt.

Chloe hesitated but, incurably honest, said, 'Yes, I'm afraid she did.'

Her heart sank further as they continued to stare at each other for a moment or two, then Ben said in grating, steely tones, 'If you cared, you wouldn't doubt me at all no matter what you'd heard about me.' He gave a bitter smile and moved towards the front door. Turning, he continued, 'Of course, we still have to work together. But as far as I can see, on a personal level, we're finished. Goodbye.' He let himself out of the door and she heard his footsteps recede along the cinder towpath.

'Goodbye,' she whispered. And with tears streaming down her face, as she for once gave way to her feelings, she made for the bedroom, flung herself down on her bed and cried her heart out.

CHAPTER NINE

ONCE back at work, Chloe found herself blessedly busy. The holiday season had started with a vengeance and she willingly did hours of overtime to cover for staff with children who wanted extra time off with their families.

She would do anything to dull the aching sense of loss she was experiencing since her traumatic parting with Ben. It was a tremendous relief to be working hard, even though it was a kind of sweet agony to see him daily at the health centre, and her heart still lurched painfully at the sight of him. One morning they met face to face just outside his office, and for a brief, magical moment their eyes met, and Chloe saw love and passion flare in his, mirroring her own feelings. They stared at each other in a breathless silence that wrapped round them like a blanket, pulling them inexorably closer and closer until, with a muttered oath, Ben turned on his heel and re-entered his room.

But generally they steered clear of each other and avoided such direct encounters, and fate kept them apart workwise. Except for a staff meeting, not once in the ensuing days did they find themselves working together.

After a week of intense loneliness and unhappiness, Chloe toyed with the idea of phoning Ben and asking him to come and talk, but something, pride perhaps, stopped her each time. What would she say if he did come? 'Are you chiefly interested in me as a proxy mother for Jemima?' Hardly: somehow it seemed wrong to broach the subject so baldly since their relationship had only just been getting off the ground when Ursula had spoilt it, and anyway he would deny it or treat such a question with cold contempt. He had been deeply hurt and enraged with her for even half believing that he could be devious—he expected that she would automatically accept that he was innocent of such deception.

If only she could make him understand that, in spite of Ursula's accusations, she didn't doubt his integrity. With all her heart she wished that she had kept her cool that afternoon when he visited *Luciana*. If she had, she could have explained that what bothered her was whether his determination to get custody of Jemima was *subconsciously* influencing his words and actions when he had spoken to her of love, and he was unaware of it. Surely he would have understood this and they would have been able to discuss the possibility rationally, but she had let that opportunity slip through her fingers by losing her temper.

There were no answers to her dilemma. She decided that she would put Ben Masters out of her mind on a personal level, and think of him only as a colleague, and start leading her own trouble-free lifestyle again. This after all was what he had proposed: that they should be civil to each other when on duty, and go their separate ways when off duty.

It was now common knowledge at the centre that Ben had a daughter who was staying with him for a holiday, who normally lived with her mother in London. This became the focus of interest for the gossips.

It hurt dreadfully that she had to learn from the

grapevine that Jemima was staying with Ben, instead of hearing it from him personally. It underlined the gulf that lay between them. And it might have been so different if she had kept her temper that afternoon. After all, Jemima had played a big part in their lives for a few short hours. But for Ursula's mischief-making, she might have been the catalyst that brought them together.

Thinking about Jemima made her wonder what he was doing to keep his daughter occupied now that he was back at work and she had only Mrs Alcot for company most of the time. Chloe felt sorry for the girl and wished that she were in a position to help enter-tain her, but immediately dismissed the half-framed thought. As things stood between her and Ben, she couldn't very well offer her services, and it was unlikely that he would ask for them.

So, though always conscious of Ben, both at home where she could see Poynters' top-floor windows from the deck of *Luciana*, and in the health centre, where they maintained cool, professional contact, life resumed something of its normal pattern.

There were the usual day-to-day happenings at the centre: regular patients turning up for regular treat-ment, interspersed with holidaymakers suffering from upset stomachs, insect bites or too much sun, and dozens of other usually minor medical problems. A high pollen count made life miserable for the asth-matics, hay fever and sinus sufferers, and doctors and nurses were kept busy administering antihistamine drugs and injections and giving advice and reassurance.

It was just as well that Chloe had at least outwardly come to terms with her feelings for Ben, for just before the end of July the Health Youth Club was due to hold its first meeting, to which they were both committed. To their relief, the schools and many of the parents had been co-operative, recognising that the club was offering supportive, not replacement, help to the youngsters. The pre-advertising aimed at the thirteen-to-sixteen age-group had been well received, but they had no idea how many people would actually turn up that evening.

The meeting, due to start at six o'clock, was to be held in the spacious play area attached to the mother and baby clinic. Chloe had been anticipating the evening with some trepidation: the thought of spending an hour or so in Ben's company made her tummy churn with a mixture of elation and anxiety. How would they react to each other, working alone together for the first time in weeks? They had met when there had been a conference to discuss the agenda for the club, but other medical and nursing staff had been present, and their head of practice had conducted the meeting.

Tonight the atmosphere was bound to be different, much more casual, and with no colleagues around. They would put on a professional front for the benefit of their young clients, but would they be able to hide their feeling from each other? There was simply no way of knowing; all she was sure about at this time was that they would both do their best to make the evening a success.

She was in the playroom tidying away toys and setting chairs in a circle, and had almost finished when Ben suddenly appeared in the doorway. He had approached very quietly along the corridor, and, though she had been expecting him, his unheralded arrival gave her a jolt. Her pulses quickened, her heart thudded painfully.

If he was affected as she was, he didn't show it. 'Good evening,' he said, in the neutral fashion he had adopted with her lately, his voice giving nothing away. 'I don't know about you, but I'm feeling a touch nervous about this meeting.' He half smiled, but the smile didn't reach his eyes.

'Yes, so am I,' replied Chloe, struggling to sound calm.

Nervous! He didn't look nervous, he looked confident and in control as always. He had taken off his tie and unbuttoned the top of his shirt. The wiry black hairs at his throat gleamed in the early evening sunlight shining through the windows.

'I just hope,' she added huskily, 'that after all your efforts to get this club off the ground, it's a fabulous success.'

'*Our* efforts, Chloe, I couldn't have got a majority consent and the wherewithal to go ahead from our colleagues without your unstinting help, and the co-operation of the schools was due entirely to your PR work.' Was it her imagination, or had his voice dropped a little as he spoke, losing its neutral quality? And had his eyes, when they met hers, lost their steel for a moment?

Chloe caught her breath. She must be imagining things. She bent down quickly and picked up the last of the scattered toys, a battered looking teddy-bear. She hugged it to her bosom, and said rather breathlessly, feeling the blood rush into her face, 'I'm glad that I was able to help—it's a great idea; it's simply got to work.'

'We can but hope and do our best,' he said laconically, with a shrug.

'Yes.' She couldn't think of anything else to say.

There was a few moments' uneasy silence, and then with long strides he crossed the room and stopped in front of her. He was very close. For one incredible moment she thought he was going to kiss her, but of course he didn't. There was an unreadable expression in his grey eyes as he looked down at her. He was so close that she could smell his aftershave and see the fine stubble on his chin. It was physically the nearest they'd been for weeks, and she suddenly found herself longing to touch his lean cheeks and smooth her fingers over his lips. She clutched the teddy harder to her, and took an involuntary step backwards.

Ben raised his eyebrows slightly as if surprised by her movement, and said in a flat, rather harsh voice, 'Chloe, I want to talk to you after the meeting's over. I have a favour to ask of you.'

'A favour?' What on earth did he mean? Why did he sound so cross? Her heart hammered uncontrollably. She repeated faintly, 'A favour?'

'A favour,' he said drily. He gave a grim little smile. 'Reluctantly, a favour from you, on Jemima's——'

Before he could say more, there was a knock at the half-open door and it was pushed wide to reveal two young girls standing uncertainly in the doorway. Chloe recognised them as the Short twins, Mandy and Beth. With a great effort, squashing all thought of her conversation with Ben, she pulled herself together and, putting on a friendly front, went forward to meet them. She introduced them to Ben, who fell easily into conversation with them.

Hot on the heels of the Short twins a group of

youngsters arrived together, three boys and four girls. Like the twins, they were slightly hesitant and uncertain of themselves, hanging back in the doorway reluctant to enter, giggling and chatting together to hide their embarrassment. Chloe drew them into the room to meet Ben. Within minutes they looked relaxed; he had the knack of talking *to* the youngsters and not down to them. It was easy to see how they might regard him as a friendly father-figure, a role model to be emulated.

For a fleeting moment, in that noisy room, with the young people gathered round Ben, it flashed into her mind that she had nothing but a bleak, childless future to look forward to. She would never have the pain or pleasure of seeing her child growing up. The odd thought came into her mind that she was glad that at least, now that she and Ben seemed to have irrevocably parted company, she would never have to tell him her suspicion that she was sterile. Somehow she knew that that would have been one of the hardest things she'd ever have to do. She could have wept. Resolutely she put her sad thoughts from her.

Her heart contracted as she looked at him talking easily with the teenagers, his austere face softened and animated. How loving he was with children and young people—no wonder he was such a good father to Jemima; no wonder he wanted custody of her.

Jemima! What had he been going to say about her before they were interrupted? And what was the favour he wanted that seemed to be connected with Jemima?

By quarter past six several more young people had arrived, and Ben called the chattering group of youngsters to order.

'The club's aim,' he explained, when they were all seated, 'is to get you fit and healthy and help you stay that way, chiefly by having sensible food and exercise, and avoiding the things that are known to be bad for you. Preventative medicine at its best. There are the obvious evils like drugs and smoking that I'm sure you've all been warned about, but there are other things too that are best avoided or taken in moderation, if you want to live a healthy lifestyle, and we will discuss them as time goes on. We're also here, Sister and I, to help you with any medical problems you may have, on an individual basis. I will see you in my consulting-room and Sister in her office if necessary at the end of each meeting. And although we are not trained counsellors, we will always listen if there are any emotional rather than physical problems that you want to talk about. Now, does anyone want to ask a question or put forward a suggestion?'

A nice-looking boy, except that his face was covered in severe acne, said, 'I'm Tim Beeching and I've got a skin problem—can you give me anything to help get rid of it? I've tried all sorts of things, but nothing's worked so far.'

Ben gave him a reassuring smile. 'Well, I think we may well be able to do something for it, Tim; there's plenty of medication around that should help.'

'Thanks.' The youth sat back in his chair looking embarrassed and triumphant at the same time. It had clearly taken some nerve to air his problem in front of an audience.

'Are we going to be weighed and have our blood-pressure taken like they do at the Well Woman clinic?' asked one of the Short twins.

'Do you think that would be a good idea?' Ben asked.

'Yes,' came a murmur from several of the group.

'Right, we'll lay that on for the next session. I suggest that you each bring a notebook with you so that you can keep track of how you're doing.'

'Brilliant,' said several of the youngsters.

'I'm Janet Sage and I want to know about food and stuff, you know, the right sort of things to eat,' said a pretty but very plump girl, blushing as she spoke. 'You see, my mum and dad don't believe in what they call fad diets, but I think we eat a lot of the wrong things at home, and that's why I'm fat. They won't take any notice of me, but they might take notice of something you suggested, Doctor.'

Ben, impressed by her courage in speaking up, said with a warm smile, 'Well, Janet, we have got a list for you to take home suggesting what foods to eat and what to avoid, and how to cook them, which your parents may find useful. They're right, of course, about crash diets being pretty useless. If they work at all it's only for a brief period and then you start putting on weight again. Much better to lose weight gradually by eating sensibly all the time and not in fits and starts. Hopefully your parents will be persuaded that this is a good idea, and you'll all benefit from the suggestions made. If it's any help, I would be happy to have a word with them.'

'Oh, great, thank you.'

The ice was now well and truly broken and questions and suggestions began coming in thick and fast. Ben fielded them with consummate ease, while Chloe, admiring his handling of the now bubbling teenagers, and ruthlessly squashing all her personal emotions, was kept busy taking notes for future reference.

Just before the session was due to end, Tim Beeching spoke up again, and asked Ben if he could do anything about his 'spots', as he referred to them, tonight.

'Certainly I can. There are lots of things that can be prescribed that might help. I'll have a good look at your face when we've finished here and I'll see what can be done about it.'

Tim looked pleased and relieved. 'That'll be great, Doctor, thanks. My dad said that you can't do anything about them, that they'll go eventually but you've just got to learn to live with them.'

'Well, we'll do our best to prove him wrong, Tim. I'll see you in my room in a few minutes.' Soon after that he brought the meeting to an end, said goodnight to everyone and thanked them for coming and for making the session so lively. He then went off, taking Tim with him, while Chloe gave out the fact sheets and steered everyone, flatteringly reluctant to leave, out into the corridor.

The first meeting of the Health Youth Club had clearly been a success.

It was very quiet in the playroom after everyone had gone, and as she went round closing windows and stacking chairs Chloe was able to give herself up to the luxury of thinking along personal lines.

An overwhelming tide of excitement suddenly welled up within her. Ben had suggested that they talk so that he might ask her a favour. It opened up all sorts of opportunities. Maybe they were not as irrevocably separated as she had thought. Perhaps she would tell him honestly how she felt—since trying not to love him had made her so miserable, why not be happy by letting him see how much she loved him and, above all, trusted him? Let matters take their course and to hell with the consequences.

What consequences? She wasn't quite sure, so she pushed them out of her mind.

At that moment Ben returned and stood in the doorway as he had earlier. 'Well, that's young Tim fixed up,' he said matter-of-factly. 'A course of anti-biotics, plus some antiseptic and healing lotions applied direct to those nasty pustules that he's got, could do the trick in time. Poor lad, his face is a mess.'

'I'm glad that you can do something for him,' replied Chloe. 'And just think, if it hadn't been for you and the health club, young Tim would have been putting up with his acne for several years if he'd listened to his father and not sought help.'

Ben smiled. 'I hadn't quite thought of it like that,' he said. 'But I suppose we can chalk up a definite plus for the evening.'

'More than one, I think. I believe Janet Sage will talk her parents round as regards diet. Poor girl, she is desperate to lose weight.'

'Let's hope she succeeds. She's a plucky girl, speaking up in front of everyone.'

'Yes, she is.'

A hushed silence fell as they looked at each other across the room. Mote-filled evening sunshine poured in through the windows. To Chloe, the hot summer air seemed full of unspoken thoughts and desires, as fragile and ethereal as the dancing motes of dust. It was unreal. There was just her and Ben in the whole. . .

Ben said briskly, shattering the moment, 'Pack up

now, Chloe. I suggest that we have a drink at the Castle Arms while I sound you out about this favour that I have to ask of you.'

It wasn't a request, it was an order.

Chloe let out a long breath. He appeared to have been completely unmoved by their silent exchange. Had she alone imagined its significance? He seemed oblivious, she thought sadly, or was he just determined to ignore it? He stood in the doorway watching her as she stacked the last chair and shut the last window. He looked remote and rather grim. How dared he order her around like a schoolgirl? A spark of anger flared up inside her. 'You don't have to sweeten me up by buying me a drink,' she said tartly. 'Just tell me what this favour is that you want from me, and I'll give you an answer here and now.'

Ben raised an eyebrow. 'It isn't a question of sweetening you up,' he said in even tones. 'I just thought that we would try to do this in a civilised manner.'

His words hurt. 'When you walked out on me on *Luciana*, you said that we were finished—no fraternising except at work, otherwise we were to go our separate ways, remember?'

'Yes, of course I remember,' he said impatiently. 'As if I could forget, and I certainly meant it, and mean it still, but circumstances force me to seek your help. I wouldn't ask anything of you for myself, but knowing you and your generosity, I feel that I can ask you for Jemima's sake.'

'For Jemima?'

'Yes, for Jemima. So please do come and have a drink while I explain. Think of it as a business rather than a social meeting if you like. We can talk more freely in the pub than here where we might be interrupted by the cleaners.'

He was quite right, the cleaners would be in at any moment, and in her heart she knew that in spite of everything she was pleased to have an excuse to be with him a little longer. 'All right,' she said. 'I'll have a drink with you while you put me in the picture. I'll just go along to my office and tidy up.'

Ben nodded. 'Good, meet you in the car park in ten minutes.'

'Fine.'

Twenty minutes or so later they were seated in the dim interior of the Castle Arms, with their drinks in front of them.

Ben looked at Chloe across the narrow table. 'About this favour,' he said crisply. 'Before I ask it, I want you to promise that you'll say no if you feel that you can't or don't want to be involved. Please don't say yes just to be accommodating. Will you promise me that?'

She nodded. 'I will.'

'Well, to explain. Tomorrow, I'm on duty or on call all day until midnight, and I'm reluctant to change my duties since I have so recently had time off to move house. Unfortunately my housekeeper has to have the day off for pressing personal reasons. She'll be back some time during the evening, but can't be sure when. I don't want Jemima to be on her own and I'd be most grateful if she could spend the day with you, Chloe— that's the favour that I have to beg.' He took another mouthful of lager and looked at her over the rim of his glass. 'I know it's a lot to ask,' he said in a low level voice, 'after all that's happened. It won't, of course, make any difference to the situation between us, but will you help a colleague in difficulties?'

Chloe took in a ragged breath. It must have been painful for him asking a favour of her; he wasn't to know that nothing would give her greater pleasure than looking after his child. She thrilled at the thought, and her heart beat faster. She didn't hesitate, but said in a steady voice, 'It'll be a pleasure looking after Jemima, Ben. I just hope that she enjoys my company as much as I feel I shall enjoy hers.'

A look of relief passed over his face, lighting up his lean, austere features for an instant. 'I don't think there's any doubt about that,' he said. He held up his glass in salute. 'Many thanks for coming to the rescue. It's a load off my mind.' He swallowed the last of his lager. 'Now would you like another drink, or shall we be on our way? I dare say you will be glad to get home—I've kept you long enough.'

She was for a moment saddened by his brusqueness, but only briefly. She could look forward to tomorrow and having Jemima with her. He quite clearly wanted to bring the evening to an end, and had meant what he'd said about the situation between them being unchanged. He had done what he could for his daughter, and there was an end to it.

She refused another drink and gathered up her shoulder-bag. Together they left the Castle Arms, wished each other a friendly but casual goodnight, and then went their separate ways.

CHAPTER TEN

CHLOE drove home, had supper and prepared for bed in a state of mild euphoria, going over and over in her mind the events of the evening. Ben's coolness and determination to maintain a distance between them, in spite of having to ask her a favour, couldn't dim her pleasure at the thought of having Jemima for the day. To have his daughter to care for was the next best thing to having Ben himself.

A *frisson* of anxiety swept over her. Supposing Jemima didn't like her, or took an instant dislike to her? Supposing she resented the fact that her father had to leave her with a near-stranger for the day? The fact that they had met briefly when she had been injured, and had forged some sort of rapport, might not weigh with her at all.

Well, that was something she would have to face tomorrow. For Ben's sake it was a challenge that she was only too ready to take on.

On this thought she eventually fell asleep.

Chloe's first thought when she woke the following morning was that today she would soon be seeing and talking to Ben again. She showered and dressed in casually smart knee-length flower-patterned trousers and a pristine loose white cotton shirt. She brushed her honey-blonde hair till it shone and fastened it back with a clip at the nape of her neck in a neat, tucked-under roll.

Her tummy churned with excitement and apprehension as she tidied the saloon, plumped up the gaily coloured cushions on the low-slung armchairs and studio couch, and arranged orange marigolds and nasturtiums in a brass bowl in the tiny hearth. Then she put coffee on to percolate and within minutes the whole boat was filled with its delicious aroma. The room glowed with colour, the furniture gleamed with polishing; there wasn't anything else she could do before her visitors were due to arrive.

From the saloon window she saw them walking along the towpath side by side, and her heart beat a familiar tattoo at the sight of Ben. He looked lean and fit in a blue open-necked shirt and grey, well tailored trousers, and Jemima looked slender and pretty in a flowery sundress.

Heart hammering, Chloe opened the front door wide as they crossed the gangplank.

'Good morning, welcome aboard,' she said.

'Thank you,' said Ben, gently pushing his daughter ahead of him into the porch. 'Jemima's been looking forward to meeting you again, Chloe, haven't you, love?'

Jemima nodded and exchanged smiles and murmured greetings with Chloe as they moved into the sitting-room.

'Thanks very much for having me,' she said in a polite little voice. 'I think it's brilliant spending the day on a houseboat. I've never been on one before.'

'Well, in some ways it's not much different from living in a house, except that there's water around you instead of a garden.'

'That's what makes it so exciting; there always seems to be so much going on on the river. I can just see some of it from my bedroom window between the trees.'

'Yes, that's true, it's pretty busy at times, but it can be quiet too. I hope you won't be bored.'

'I'm sure I won't be.'

They smiled at each other again, and Jemima's grey eyes were warm and bright like Ben's when he was dealing with children. With a rush of relief and pleasure, Chloe sensed that it was going to be all right. Ben's daughter liked her; they had taken instinctively to each other.

They both turned to look at Ben, who had stood a little aside as if purposely giving them a moment to talk together.

He said rather brusquely, 'Well, now that you two have met properly, I'd better be off—big list this morning. Thanks for having Jemima, Chloe.'

'A pleasure. Won't you stay for coffee?'

He shook his head. 'No, thank you, I must get on.' He kissed Jemima goodbye and moved to the door. 'May I call in at the end of the morning and see how things are going?'

'Of course, and why not stay and have lunch?' said Chloe impulsively, surprising herself, for she hadn't meant to ask him.

Ben frowned. 'Thank you, but I think not,' he said in a voice devoid of expression, reminding her with a hard, piercing look how things stood between them. 'I'm not sure when I'll be finishing my visits, and I plan to catch up with some paperwork over the lunch hour.'

Chloe drew in her breath sharply as a stab of pain went through her. He had rebuffed her in no uncertain terms, making it clear how he felt. She was a fool to have asked him.

Jemima, oblivious of the crackling vibes passing between the adults, pleaded, 'Oh, Dad, do come, it'll be lovely for us all to have lunch together.'

Ben looked down at her vibrant face, and the expression on his own softened. Chloe had never seen him so hesitant. 'Well, Jem, I don't know. . .'

'Please.'

Unable to resist her, he capitulated. 'All right, if Chloe doesn't mind keeping lunch should I be late. . .?' He gave Chloe a questioning look.

'Of course I don't. We'll expect you when we see you.' Her heart lurched with pleasure at the prospect, in spite of his reluctance.

With the ghost of a smile for Jemima's benefit, he nodded, and said pleasantly, 'Right, hopefully see you about oneish.'

Chloe and Jemima stood outside the front porch and watched him stride over the gangplank and along the towpath towards Poynters, where he turned and waved before disappearing through the garden gate.

Jemima had fallen in love with *Luciana* on sight, and begged to be allowed to see everything, from sundeck to bathroom.

'I'd like to live on a houseboat when I'm older,' she announced when they finished the tour and were seated at the bar that divided the galley from the main saloon, while Chloe served coffee. 'I think I'll ask Daddy to buy me one one day,' she said thoughtfully. 'I'd like a home of my own and it would be more fun than a flat.'

'They're not cheap, you know, good houseboats,' Chloe explained. 'Especially at moorings like this.'

'I expect Daddy could afford it,' said Jemima confidently.

'Oh, well, in that case, if you haven't changed your mind in the next few years, I can honestly recommend living on the water. It's a wonderful way of life, especially if you have good neighbours as I have,' said Chloe. 'Which reminds me—the Lowell family, who are friends of mine, are back in residence. There's six of them, and two of the girls are about your age. They own the houseboat right at the far end, and come down several times a year for holidays. I'll take you along to meet them this afternoon, if you would like that.'

'Sounds brilliant.'

'Right, we'll do that. Now, what about helping me to get lunch ready? We're having melon for starters, and cold lamb with a tossed salad and jacket potatoes to follow, and ice-cream and fruit for pudding.'

'Great. What can I do to help?'

'Any good at scrubbing potatoes?'

'Of course, I often do them for Mrs Alcot.'

'Right, then get going on these,' said Chloe, tipping potatoes into a bowl, 'while I see to the salad and dice the melon.'

After they had finished preparing the lunch, they sat on the sundeck and chatted as they watched the small sailboats and bigger holiday craft tack up and down the river. Chloe was amazed and pleased at how easily they talked to each other; they seemed to have no inhibitions. She realised that, if she cared to, she could encourage Jemima to talk about her parents and their life at home before they split up. It was tempting to find out more about Ben, but she didn't try—it would have been too much like spying. Instead, she got Jemima to talk about school and her hopes and ambitions.

'Do you know yet what you want to do when you leave school or university?' she asked.

'Yes,' said Jemima eagerly. 'I want to be a teacher and teach small children.' Her face fell. 'But my mother doesn't want me to do anything. She says that I should stay at home till I get married, there's no need for me to go to work. She doesn't seem to realise that I want to work.'

'And your father, what does he say?'

'That I should go ahead and train to be a teacher if that's what I want to do, and he will give me his support.'

'And are you going to do that?'

Jemima turned her delicate, heart-shaped face towards Chloe, her grey eyes, so like her father's, bright and intense. 'Do you think I should?'

A great wave of affection for this lovely girl swept over Chloe. She felt that she had known her for a long time, but was conscious that she must answer carefully, and in no way aggravate the situation between her parents. She said cautiously, 'I think you should have guidance from your careers teacher at school, and then do what you think is right for you. If you explain properly, I'm sure your mother will understand that you want to do a worthwhile job. But at the end of the day it must be your decision; it's your future.'

'But if it was up to you, if I were your daughter, for instance, you would say go ahead, wouldn't you?'

Chloe's heart bumped: her daughter, Ben's daughter. Her mind raced. She said truthfully, 'Yes, if that was what you wanted to do, I would say press on and work hard to achieve your goal.'

'Then that's what I shall do,' said Jemima decisively.

Chloe squashed her qualms; she had done her best to be even-handed. The girl deserved encouragement. She said warmly, 'Then I wish you good luck. I'm sure you'll make a splendid teacher. Your father's great with children; you've probably inherited his talent.'

'Oh, I hope so,' said Jemima fervently.

With surprise, Chloe realised that it was nearly one o'clock. The morning had flown past, and it was time to put the finishing touches to lunch. Jemima laid the table on the sundeck while Chloe put the potatoes in the microwave to bake, gave the salad a final toss, and arranged the chilled melon with a squeeze of lemon in glass dishes.

She was still in the galley and Jemima up on deck when Ben arrived at ten past one. His sudden appearance in the porch rattled her and she had to take a deep breath to steady herself.

'Oh, hello,' she said with a calm that she was far from feeling. 'You made good time.'

'Got through my list quicker than expected. How have things gone this morning? Is Jemima all right?'

'She's fine; we've talked about everything under the sun as if we'd known each other for ages.'

'She's needed someone to talk to, a female confidante. Thank you.'

'No need for thanks,' she said briskly. 'I've enjoyed the morning. Jemima's a lovely girl and easy to entertain. Now what would you like to drink—a dry sherry or something else?'

'A dry sherry would be just right.'

She poured two glasses of pale gold liquid. Their

fingers touched as she handed him his glass. She shivered and turned hastily back to the microwave. Had he noticed? The accidental touch had taken her by surprise. It was electric. His magnetism was as strong as ever. Mentally she shook herself—she mustn't let him affect her. He had made it crystal-clear how he felt about her. She must remember that he was here on sufferance, as it were, for his daughter's sake. He had asked a favour of her only as a last resort. His feelings for her were dead, and she mustn't let *her* feelings show and spoil their lunch party.

In an impersonal voice, Ben asked, 'Anything that I can do to help?'

'Please, take the melons up to the sundeck. Jemima's there laying the table.'

Left alone for a few minutes, she pulled herself together. She would secretly enjoy the fact that the three of them were on *Luciana*, sharing a meal together like a family, and try to ignore the underlying tension between her and Ben.

Lunch in fact turned out to be a success, chiefly on account of Jemima's almost non-stop conversation about her plans for the future, and their immediate plans for the afternoon.

'Chloe's going to introduce me to the Lowell family; they're friends of hers,' she told her father. 'There's six of them, and two of the girls are about my age. They're here on holiday. Isn't it brilliant?'

'Brilliant,' agreed Ben drily. 'I'm delighted that you are going to meet someone of your own age.' He raised his glass to Jemima and then to Chloe. 'Here's to friendship,' he said with a smile.

Was there a double meaning in his words? Chloe wondered as she raised her glass and smiled in return.

Was he reminding her that the most she could hope for from him was friendship? His mouth smiled, but his eyes were unreadable, dark pools of cool grey.

Jemima said cheerfully, 'I'll take the plates down to the galley and fetch the coffee, shall I, Chloe?'

Chloe nodded. 'Please.' She felt languid and relaxed after the meal and wine.

It was very quiet after Jemima had gone, the river afternoon siesta-quiet. The water rippled gold in the bright sunshine, and the poplars began casting their welcoming shade across the deck.

Neither of them spoke. Peace and near-silence wrapped round them. Bees hummed softly in the honeysuckle. Ben leaned back in his comfortable garden chair. His eyelids drooped, his hawk-like features relaxed. Chloe feasted her eyes on him.

Suddenly the peace was shattered as a crowd of noisy children appeared at the end of the previously empty towpath. Shrill voices and laughter echoed over the sunlit water.

Slowly Ben opened his eyes and sighed. 'Kids,' he said with a groan. 'What noisy creatures they are.'

'Yes, aren't they just?' she agreed heartily, inwardly cursing them for disturbing her precious moment alone with Ben.

The children drew nearer and the noise grew louder. The voices in the quiet of the afternoon suddenly sounded very clear. Somebody shouted, 'Don't do that, you'll push us in.'

Another voice jeered, 'What, frightened of a little bit of water?'

The first voice shrieked. 'I'm not, but Kev's only little. . . Stop it, *stop it*.' Suddenly there was a dull thud and a loud splash followed by a deathly silence.

'My God,' said Ben. 'One of them has fallen in.' He leapt out of his chair and in a few strides reached the stairs. A split second later Chloe was following him, down the stairs and along the towpath to where seven or eight children were grouped on the grass verge opposite the houseboat next door but one to *Luciana*. Most of them were standing shocked and silent, staring down into the space between the boat and the bank, but three children were lying on the bank stretching their hands down into the water.

Ben pushed through the group of frightened young-sters and stared down into the dark water. It was quite empty, stagnant, still except for the ripples that the children were making.

'Where did he fall in?' he asked sharply.

One of the bigger children lying on the bank pointed with a shaking finger. 'About there,' she quavered. 'Get him out, it's my brother—he hit his head on the boat as he fell in.'

'Know how deep it is?' Ben asked Chloe.

'About eight feet, I think, but I'm not sure.'

Ben nodded and, taking off his shoes, lowered himself into the water near where the child had fallen in. When the water came up to his neck, he took a deep breath and half ducked, half dived down into the depths, until only his feet and legs were visible, kicking about beneath the murky surface.

Chloe and the stunned children watched in breath-less silence. It seemed an age, but was less than a minute before he came up again, holding in his arms a small, limp form.

'Oh, Kev,' said the boy's sister, and burst into tears.

Chloe took the child from Ben and laid him on the bank on his back with his head turned to one side.

Water gushed out of his mouth. There was a bruise on one side of his forehead. She thought that he was probably concussed. She opened the child's mouth wide and scooped out some slimy weed, checked his heartbeat and his breathing—she couldn't feel or hear anything.

She shook her head as Ben hauled himself out of the water and knelt down on the other side of the boy. 'Mouth to mouth and nose,' he said urgently. 'I'll support him and do the breathing, you do the chest compression—he's small, one hand only.'

He tilted the boy's head backwards to free the airways, then placed his mouth over the child's mouth and nose and gave the initial four quick, gentle puffs. There was no response. The small chest remained ominously still. Chloe placed the heel of her hand lightly on the narrow chest and began compressing gently. For a child, apply fifteen light, quick compressions to two ventilations, she recalled automatically. Ben bent his head and breathed into the small body, two puffs, compressions, check for response. There was none. Chloe repeated the compressions. Ben inflated again, and again. Nothing. They carried on rhythmically: inflate, compress, inflate, compress.

It seemed an endless time before there was any response, then suddenly the small chest heaved as air began to get into the boy's lungs, and he spluttered and coughed and took in a shuddering breath.

A concerted sigh and a murmur went round the group of onlookers, swelled now by passers-by, some nearby neighbours of Chloe's, and Jemima, who was standing with her arms round Kevin's sister.

Relief swamped them, and for one fleeting, magical moment Ben and Chloe stared triumphantly into each other's eyes over the small, vulnerable body that lay between them. The child was alive! They had saved him. For that fraction of a moment, they were oblivious to everyone around them. Ben's eyes glowed, soft and tender. He seemed to embrace her with a look. Or was she imagining it?

He said softly, 'Thank you, I think we've pulled it off.' Quickly he examined the boy's eyes and took his pulse. 'Pupils normal, pulse a bit erratic but volume good. I don't think he's badly concussed. The bruise and contusion on his forehead are superficial. With luck he'll be coming round soon, but we'd better put him into recovery until he does.' They turned the boy on to his left side in the recovery position.

Kevin's sister knelt down beside him. 'Can I touch him?' she asked.

'Do,' said Ben, 'and talk to him. The sooner we can bring him round, the better.' He turned to the crowd. 'Has anybody phoned for an ambulance?'

'Yes, it's on its way,' said Jenny Blake, the owner of *Rosalea*, the houseboat where the accident had happened. 'And will this help, Chloe?' she added, handing over a blanket. 'Or do you want to bring him inside?'

'No, we won't move him as the ambulance is on its way,' Ben said, as he helped Chloe wrap Kevin in the blanket. 'This will do fine. But can you get some more details about young Kevin here? His full name and address, and a phone number if possible, so that his parents can be informed about what's happened.'

'Will do.' Jenny was only too pleased to be useful. She quickly learned from one of the bigger boys that they were all staying at the local holiday camp. The injured boy was Kevin Taylor, his elder sister who was with him was Vikki. Jenny offered to phone the camp and break the news of what had happened to the Taylors. Her offer was accepted. Shortly afterwards she returned to report that, after their initial shock, Mr and Mrs Taylor had responded well to the situation. They were coming at once to the scene of the accident, and would arrange for the parents of the other children involved to be alerted.

A short while later the ambulance arrived. It had to park at the end of the towpath, which was too narrow to take a vehicle.

The paramedics took over from Ben and Chloe. They worked quickly and efficiently, talking to Kevin, making sure his airways were clear and administering oxygen. They were putting him on to the stretcher when his eyes flickered open, and after a few puzzled moments, when he didn't know where he was, he had regained consciousness enough to recognise his sister and speak to her.

'Kevin, we're going to take you to the ambulance now,' said one of the paramedics. 'Just keep talking to Vikki.'

There was quite a little procession along the towpath. Vikki walked beside the stretcher, with Ben, Chloe and Jemima following and the other children and some onlookers trailing behind.

Kevin was being loaded into the ambulance when his parents, and other parents connected with the children, arrived on the scene.

The Taylors were of course extremely anxious, and Ben did his best to reassure them. He explained that Kevin had responded well to initial treatment, and that further treatment would be carried out in hospital.

A few minutes later Ben, Chloe and Jemima watched as the ambulance, followed by the Taylors, drove away. As suddenly as it had begun, their part in the emergency had finished. They were no longer responsible for the small boy who had so nearly drowned. He was safe now in other hands.

They walked slowly back along the towpath, with Jemima walking a little ahead of them. They both felt physically and mentally drained. Ben took one of Chloe's hands in his and squeezed it gently. Low as she was, at his touch her pulses raced.

'Are you all right?' he asked softly, and his eyes, luminous and tender, searched her face. Was he remembering that magic moment when Kevin had taken his first tentative, ragged breath?

'I'm fine, thanks, relieved that it's all over and that the little boy is safe. He looked so helpless when you first brought him out of the river.'

'Yes, didn't he? I wondered for a moment if we would be able to pull him through. Children in distress always seem so specially vulnerable, don't they? A reminder of how short and fragile life is.'

'Yes, I feel that.'

'Do you?' He lowered his voice. 'Chloe, we need to talk.'

'Do we?' Her voice trembled a little.

'Oh, yes, we must sort out matters between us. These last few weeks have been hell.'

'They have for me. I didn't think you cared, you looked so. . .so *hard*.'

'Oh, Chloe, if only you knew. . . But I was shattered to think that you seemed to believe Ursula rather than me.' He stopped walking, and turned to face her as they reached Jenny's houseboat. Jemima was already on the foredeck, talking animatedly to Jenny and a girl of about her own age. Ben said quickly, 'I'll ring you later. We have to work this out.'

Her heart beat faster. 'I want to desperately,' she said. Then she added in her practical fashion, 'You should go and change out of those wet clothes.'

He smiled ruefully. 'Indeed I should.' He looked at his watch, and his mouth quirked at the corner in a small smile. 'Just time before afternoon surgery. I'll go straight home. Say goodbye to Jem for me.'

He walked, with long, deliberate strides along the towpath toward Poynters and Chloe crossed the gangplank to *Rosalea*.

CHAPTER ELEVEN

HALF an hour later Chloe was back on board *Luciana*, alone.

Jenny had persuaded her to let her take Jemima, together with her niece Lucy, to the leisure centre where she was meeting some friends. 'The girls seem to have taken to each other, and there will be other young people in the party. It should be fun for both of them. Of course, you could join us too—the more the merrier. Do say yes.'

Chloe begged off on her own account, pleading a headache. She certainly felt a bit muzzy-headed, probably a reaction to the emotional and physical effort she had made in helping to resuscitate little Kevin. But the real reason she refused the invitation, she acknowledged to herself, was because she suddenly felt the need to be on her own and have time to think. She could do this with a clear conscience, provided that Jemima was happy, and she was certainly that; she was bubbling over with enthusiasm at the prospect of going to the leisure centre with Lucy.

For a moment Chloe hesitated on Jemima's behalf, wondering if Ben would approve. She decided that he would. He had briefly met Jenny, and knew that she was a responsible woman. And Lucy seemed a nice girl; he would be only too pleased that Jemima had found someone of her own age with whom to make friends.

But a tiny niggle of doubt assailed her now that she

was on her own. Would he be angry to learn that she had handed Jemima over into somebody else's care? Would he misconstrue the situation and think that she had got tired of looking after his daughter? Well, there was no point in speculating about his reaction; best let him know straight away what had happened.

She picked up the phone and dialled the health centre and got through to Ben immediately. He was between patients. When he answered, she told him quickly what had happened.

'Oh, that's great,' he said. 'Jem will enjoy being with other people of her own age. Thanks for fixing it.'

'You don't mind that I didn't go?'

'Not at all. You need a breather after a morning with my chatterbox of a daughter, not to mention the accident. After all, it is supposed to be your day off. Take it easy, try to relax.'

'Will do.'

She was about to say goodbye and put the phone down, when he said softly, 'Chloe, if you're on your own, we could talk, could we not?'

'You know that I want to end this silence between us,' she breathed, her heart thumping, 'but what have we got to talk about?'

'You and me and our future,' he said bluntly. 'We mustn't let Ursula spoil everything for us. That's what we've been doing. Let's get things sorted out. I'll see you when surgery's finished. I'll be on call, but who knows? We might be lucky and have a quiet evening. Goodbye.' He put the phone down before she could say another word.

She stood still as a statue for some minutes after he had rung off. His words and his rather abrupt attitude had stunned her. Our future, he'd said, as if there was no doubt that they had a future together. What did he mean by that? He had seemed to imply that if the malicious Ursula had not interfered, their relationship would have matured weeks ago? But would it? Yes, it was no use deceiving herself, she was utterly and completely in love with Ben, and had been since she first met him. Ursula's appearance and innuendoes had only slowed up, not stopped, her love for him. And Ben must feel the same. That was why he wanted to talk. He loved her as she loved him. He was ready to forgive her doubting him. Her heart seemed to turn over, her breathing almost stop. But why now, so suddenly, when only this morning he'd been cold and distant. . .? Of course, it was on account of that fleeting moment when their eyes had met over the small body of the nearly drowned boy. It put things into perspective, a reminder that life was short, precious. If she was not imagining it, and she was sure that she was not, his eyes then had told her that he loved her. She was convinced now that he had not deceived her, not even unconsciously. If he wanted her, it was for herself, and not to provide Jemima with a proxy mother as Ursula had suggested.

So he loved her. So he might want to marry her. Marry! Her heart soared—and then plummeted. He had been and would be totally honest with her, but could she say the same for herself? Her long-held suspicion that she might be infertile fought its way once more from where she had pushed it to the back of her mind, suddenly resuming an overwhelming importance. If Ben did ask her to marry him, how could she accept without telling him that she might not be able to give him more children? But then he might either reject her, or marry her out of pity. And she wouldn't be able to bear that.

A sob caught in her throat—what the hell was she going to do? Happiness was within her grasp, a life of loving with Ben, and yet further away than it had ever been.

Her head was aching badly now—she must get a drink and take a couple of aspirin. If Ben was coming later she must be clear-headed, and know exactly what she was going to say to him. She must stop him from putting himself in a position from which he couldn't back out. She must be honest with him whatever the cost.

As in a dream she went through to the galley, poured herself some orange juice, took it up to the sundeck and lay down on a comfortable lounger. Tears trickled silently down her cheeks and she dashed them away with an impatient hand. She mustn't feel sorry for herself. She had rebuilt her life once before after a failed marriage, and if necessary, she could do it again, even if it meant leaving the job she loved and her beloved *Luciana*.

At last, worn out by emotion, she dozed off in the dappled shade of the poplar trees. Suddenly, half awake, she became aware of somebody sitting in the chair beside her. She opened her eyes wide and struggled into a sitting position. 'Ben,' she murmured in a strangled voice which she fought to keep steady. 'I wasn't expecting you yet. Surely you should still be working?'

'Well, I finished my afternoon list early, and decided that my paperwork could wait. Our meeting and talking was more important, especially as I have received an interesting phone call from Ursula.'

'Ursula!'

'Yes.' He didn't elaborate, but said softly, 'You know, you look very vulnerable when you are asleep. But tell me, why have you been crying?' He touched her tearstained cheek with a long index finger and her whole being trembled.

She brushed his hand away. 'Don't, I can't tell you,' she said sharply, turning her head away. How *could* she resist him, how *could* she bring herself to say what she must and perhaps finish their relationship forever?

With a very firm hand he caught hold of her chin and turned her to face him. She lowered her beautiful emerald-green eyes, brilliant with unshed tears, so that they didn't have to meet his luminous grey ones. Her dark-tipped, honey-coloured lashes curled on her high cheekbones. 'Why not?' he asked in a low, urgent voice. 'Why can't you tell me? If it's something to do with us, then I've a right to know, and if it's not to do with us, then I *want* to know so that I can support you. You're not a weepy woman, so there must be a sound reason why you've been crying.'

He was right. She owed him honesty. She had to tell him. Now was the moment. Slowly she opened her eyes and met his. 'Not here,' she said, conscious of the nearby towpath. 'Let's go downstairs.'

'Right,' he said, 'as you wish.' He offered her a warm, strong hand and pulled her to her feet.

He preceded her down the steps to the lower deck, but stood back so that she could enter the saloon in front of him. She felt the magnetism flowing out from him as she passed, and sensed that he wanted to take her into his arms, but was deliberately holding back. For a moment she wished that he *would* take her in his arms and make all her fears disappear. His nearness was a torment. Brushing against his blue-shirted chest, which seemed to emphasise his strength and masculinity, she made herself hurry past, straight through the saloon to the galley.

She must do something with her hands. 'Tea,' she suggested breathlessly.

'Please.'

'How do you want it?' she heard herself ask in a high, strained voice.

'China with lemon,' he replied, seating himself at the breakfast bar on the high stool and resting his feet on the rung of another stool.

He watched her as she pottered around.

She avoided his eyes, plugged in the kettle, got out the packet of China tea, and sliced the lemon. She knew she was playing for time, but how to begin? How to tell him what she had to? Baldly? —Ben, if you were thinking of asking me to marry you, don't, because there's a good possibility I can't have children. Ridiculous. Out of chivalry, the very thing she least wanted, he would propose. But how else?

Ben spoke softly, jerking her out of her reverie. 'Chloe, love, you're all tensed up and I can almost hear you trying to sort out your muddled thoughts. Shall I go first with my news? It will cheer you up, and—who knows?—it might even help resolve the problem that's going round and round in your dear little head.'

Chloe stared at him for a moment as if he were a stranger and then very carefully poured the pale scented tea into porcelain mugs. She added a half-slice of lemon and pushed the delicate mug across the counter. A feeling of *déjà-vu* washed over her. Surely she had done all this before. China tea, the fragrant scent—good news—bad news. . .

She felt quite faint. She clutched at the counter. 'Ben,' she whispered, as she felt her knees give way.

He was round the bar in a flash and caught her in his arms as she sagged to the floor.

When she came round a few minutes later, she was lying on the sofa in the saloon with her feet propped up. Ben was kneeling beside her, rubbing her cold hands gently between his warm ones.

'That's better,' he said as her eyes flickered open. 'What brought that on—too much sun, or have you got this summer flu bug that's going round?'

'Neither, I don't know why I fainted. . . I just felt queer.' But even as she said it, she realised why. It was remembering Mark. Mark had told her that he was leaving her for another woman one evening as they were drinking China tea. The night he'd died.

But she had made China tea dozens of times since his death without it affecting her, so why had it upset her now? Of course—the answer came to her like a bolt out of the blue—it was because she had been thinking of marriage and babies, or not being able to have babies. Or was it because for a moment Ben and Mark had merged into one, both dissatisfied men, both let down by her because she couldn't have children?

It was hopeless; she couldn't marry Ben, she loved him too much.

To her fury, she was speechless, and tears started into her eyes and ran down her cheeks. Ben fished out a large white handkerchief from his trouser pocket and tenderly wiped her tears away. He kissed her damp cheeks.

'Listen, love,' he said quietly. 'Won't you tell me what's wrong? Perhaps I can help.'

She shook her head and then, a bit hysterically, gave a little hiccupping giggle. 'No, *you* can't help, not yet anyway. But I'm feeling better now, and I will tell you what I must presently—just give me some time to pull myself together.'

Ben said quietly, 'Then I shall give you my news; that should cheer you a little.' He looked down at her, his grey eyes full of love and compassion. 'Who knows? If you still have any doubts as to my intentions towards you, it will set your mind at rest.'

She looked up at him with tear-drenched eyes and swallowed.

'But I haven't any doubts about you or your intentions, Ben,' she said in a small but firm voice. 'On the contrary, I trust you implicitly.'

'Thanks for that,' he replied with quiet satisfaction. 'Now as to my news: I've heard from Ursula, telling me that she is willing for me to take over custody of Jemima, provided that she can see her frequently. Apparently, now that she means to marry again, and her future husband travels abroad constantly and she aims to go with him, Jem would be a bit of a problem.'

'Oh, Ben, I'm so pleased for you,' Chloe said, her voice spontaneously warm and eager. 'But why on earth did she have to be so bitchy when she came down here, and say that she was going to fight you for custody—she must have known then that this might happen?'

'Well, sadly, that's Ursula's style. It's in her nature to make difficulties, especially where I'm concerned. I just hope that all the wrangling over the last few years hasn't done Jem any deep damage. She needs stability.'

'And you'll give her that, Ben, and I think she knows it. She's fallen in love with Poynters and Chidhurst and being with you. Now she can have the best of both worlds: you as her anchor and her mother from time to time. I think you've solved Jem's problems, Ben. She loves both you and Ursula, but you represent safety and security as well as love, and that's what she needs. I think she is going to be a very happy girl when you break the news to her.'

'Yes, I think that's true. She needs what I can give her, and I can give her even more with your support, Chloe. I believe you've already established a rapport with her, and I'm absolutely certain that she will grow to love you as I love you. And you must know,' he said very softly, so unlike the cool, reserved man that he could be, 'that you are everything that I love about Chidhurst. We will both love you, Jem and I. The three of us will make a splendid family. Let's make it a permanent one; let's get married.' He dropped a kiss on her forehead, uncoiled himself from his semi-sitting, semi-kneeling position by the sofa, and stood up in one smooth movement.

He looked down at her from his great height, his lean but powerful frame silhouetted against the bright, early evening light streaming in through the saloon window.

Chloe stared up at him for a moment in silence, feeling the blood coming and going in her cheeks. He had proposed! The words that she had both wanted and yet dreaded to hear had been spoken. Slowly, her eyes still on his face, she swung her legs down from the end of the sofa and sat up straight. She squared her shoulders.

'B—Ben,' she said at last in a small, cracked voice, 'I don't think I can marry you.'

Ben raised his eyebrows, frowned, and then sat down beside her. He took one of her hands in his and stroked it. 'But why not? You're in love with me, and you know that I'm mad with love for you, don't you?' he said gently.

Chloe nodded.

'Then why can't you marry me? You're a free woman; I'm a free man. We're in love with each other. Surely that's all that matters?'

Making a tremendous effort, Chloe pulled herself together. In a low and remarkably steady voice considering the strain she was under, she said, 'No, that is not all that matters, Ben.'

Ben gave her a puzzled look.

The moment had come; she couldn't prevaricate further. She felt tears of pain and frustration prick at her eyelids. How would he react to what she had to say? Through clenched teeth she ground out in a voice full of resignation, 'I don't think I can have children and, knowing that, I don't expect you to want to marry me. Not that I would marry you anyway. I'm not going to spoil another life.'

There was a moment's silence. And then Ben said in a low, even voice, 'You've had all the tests?'

Chloe floundered. 'Well, no, but we tried for almost two years to have a child and nothing happened.'

'And was he all right, your husband; did he have a good and active sperm count?'

'I don't know. He didn't see anyone; we just tried.'

'Did either of you have any tests at all?'

'No, my doctor said it was too soon. He examined me and asked me a few questions, and said that everything appeared to be normal. He said he would review things when we'd been trying for a full two years. But that never happened, of course. . .'

He slid an arm along the back of the sofa and squeezed her shoulder gently and said, in a rather surprised voice as if he couldn't believe what he was hearing, 'And is this what you have been worrying about—the fact that you might or might not be able to have children? Do you really think that makes any difference to us, to my love for you?'

Chloe turned to look at him, an incredulous expression on her face. 'Doesn't it?' she whispered.

'Of course it damn well doesn't. It's you I love and want to marry, not a baby machine. Naturally I hope we'll be able to have a family, but it's not going to break my heart if we don't.' He took her into his arms and kissed her slowly and gently on her mouth and rubbed his cheek against hers. 'To be fanciful,' he said softly, 'my heart will only break if you refuse to marry me. We'll have each other, we've got Jemima, and there's such a thing as adoption, although I have a hunch that that's not going to be necessary. There's absolutely nothing to indicate that you can't conceive, and if it turns out that there is, we'll get the best advice on the market.'

'But you love children. It'll make you dreadfully unhappy if we can't have them.'

'No it won't, for all the reasons that I've given already. 'Listen, love——' he put both his hands on her shoulders and shook her slightly '—you've got things all out of proportion because of what happened to Mark, and his death is linked with your thinking

that you can't have children. But there is no corre-
lation between the two. He had an accident. That
could have happened at any time, for any reason.'

Chloe shook her head. 'No, it couldn't, it happened
because he got drunk, and he got drunk because he
had to tell me that he was leaving me. And he was
leaving me because I couldn't give him a child and I
made such a scene and he stormed out of the house.'
She hid her face in her hands.

'Did he tell you that he was leaving you because
you couldn't have a child?'

'No. He said that he was in love with another
woman,' she said in a muffled voice.

Ben took both her numbed, trembling hands in his.
'Chloe, however much it hurts, you must accept that
as being true. Mark left you, as Ursula left me,
because he was fickle. He fell out of love with you and
into love with somebody else. It happens. It had
absolutely nothing to do with your not having a baby.
In fact, I would hazard a guess that he would have
looked on a baby as a liability.'

'Do you really think that?' she whispered.

'Yes, I do,' he confirmed without hesitation.

'Oh, Ben,' she murmured. She felt as if a huge
weight had been lifted from her. She closed her eyes
for a moment, then opened them wide and looked
directly into his. 'I do love you,' she said. 'Hold me
close. Please show me that you love me.'

His warm grey eyes looked steadily into hers. 'Will
you marry me,' he asked, 'as soon as I can make the
arrangements?'

'I will,' she said.

'In that case. . .' He scooped her up in his arms

without ceremony and carried her across the saloon to the bedroom door.

'You're sure about this?' he said as they reached it.

'Quite sure. Please make love to me.'

Ben pushed open the door. 'I will,' he said, as he laid her down tenderly on the wide double bed that almost filled the forward berth.

'You'd better pull the curtains to,' Chloe said softly. 'We're quite close to the towpath.'

'And the last thing we want is an audience,' said Ben as he drew together the rosebud curtains at the casement windows of the rounded bow of the boat, and shut out the brilliant sunlight. The room was bathed in a golden-pink glow.

He stood looking down at her as he slowly removed his shirt and then his trousers and his brief pants. The tanned muscles of his torso and thighs with their thatch of dark hair rippled in the soft light, contrasting with the paleness of his loins and his erect penis and triangle of black, curling hair. His sheer physical strength and masculinity seemed to fill the cabin.

Chloe's heart pounded. 'Oh, Ben,' she said breathlessly, 'you're beautiful.'

'Hey, that's my line,' he said with a sardonically raised eyebrow and a small chuckle.

He bent and kissed her gently, and then with steady, careful fingers unbuttoned her blouse and slid it off her shoulders. He touched her bare breasts fleetingly with his lips as he unzipped her trousers and eased them down over her slender hips. His eyes swept over her as she lay there naked, a pale ribbon across the bed, waiting for him, hardly breathing, her honey-blonde hair spread like a fan round her head.

'My God, but you're lovely,' he said hoarsely. His eyes were large and dark with passion.

He knelt on the bed and gently nudged her legs apart until he was kneeling between them. He stroked her hair, running his fingers through it and lifting the golden strands and letting them fall back on the pillow. Softly his lips and long fingers trailed down the line of her cheeks and chin and neck, and then he cupped both her breasts with his hands and brought his mouth down on her nipples and teased them with his tongue until they were hard and erect. Chloe moaned with pleasure and arched herself against him, and he lifted his head and moved upwards until his lips met hers, stretching his full length so that the whole weight of his body was upon her. Her thighs felt heavy as slowly and gently he rubbed his hard flesh against her soft moistness. She arched again, moaned again, and began moving rhythmically with him, and suddenly, smoothly, he was inside her, hard and throbbing.

Their bodies moved in unison in an ecstasy of awareness and delight, straining to get closer and closer, until at last, magically, they climaxed at the same moment.

They lay breathless and shuddering for several minutes still locked together. Then Ben kissed her gently and rolled on to his side, taking her with him, his strong brown arms holding her close. For a few moments they lay silent and content, looking into each other's eyes as the quiet of the room washed around them.

A slight breeze ruffled the rosebud curtains, throwing ripples of golden-pink light over the bed; scent from the honeysuckle that framed the window wafted through the room. Familiar sounds, both near and distant, reached them, touched them, dreamlike: the shrill shouts of children, footsteps on the towpath, the gentle lapping of water against the boat.

Ben ran his long fingers through her golden hair and brought a strand to his lips and kissed it. 'Such beautiful hair,' he murmured. 'And you are so beautiful, so loving and warm, and yet you look so cool and serene. A sort of ice maiden.' He gave a deep rumbling chuckle and rubbed her small, neat nose with his formidable aquiline one. He kissed her gently. 'An ice maiden whom I've succeeded in melting.'

Chloe said with a little laugh, 'Oh, Ben, you're a fine one to talk about being distant, my darling. You were so austere and unapproachable when you first came to Chidhurst, I thought that I'd never get to know you.'

'Did you want to get to know me?' he asked softly, his lips teasing hers as he spoke.

'Oh, yes, though I pretended at first that I didn't.' She caught his hand and kissed the palm, and continued to hold it against her lips. 'I love you,' she said softly.

'And I you,' he said tenderly. 'With all my heart, and making love to you was wonderful.'

'Was it?' she whispered.

'Yes, because we truly love each other, we're each of us trying to give, which is something I suspect neither of us has experienced before from our previous partners.'

'True love!'

'True love,' he smiled. 'We'll be friends and colleagues as well as lovers,' he promised in his deep, melodious voice. 'Life will take on a new meaning.' His mouth quirked endearingly in his inimitable lopsided smile. 'I love you with all my heart, Sister Chloe Lucas, and I know you love me, that's enough to be going on with for now.'

'Yes, Doctor, you're no longer a stranger,' Chloe murmured under her breath.

'What did you say?' asked Ben.

'I love you,' said Chloe with a dimpling smile.

'Good,' replied Ben, pulling her closer to him. 'Because I love you, and I mean to prove it. . .again.'

10th anniversary Temptation is Ten!

Join the festivities as Mills & Boon celebrates Temptation's tenth anniversary in February 1995.

There's a whole host of in-book competitions and special offers with some great prizes to be won—watch this space for more details!

In March, we have a sizzling new mini-series Lost Loves about love lost...love found. And, of course, the Temptation range continues to offer you fun, sensual exciting stories all year round.

After ten tempting years, nobody can resist

Temptation **10th anniversary**

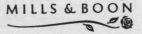